Annie's Quilted Mysteries™

UNSAVORY
NOTIONS

AMY LILLARD

Annie's®
AnniesFiction.com

Library of Congress-in-Publication Data
Unsavory Notions / by Amy Lillardy
p. cm.
I. Title
                 2014942581

AnniesFiction.com
800-282-6643
Annie's Quilted Mysteries
Series Creator: Shari Lohner
Series Editors: Shari Lohner, Janice Tate, and Ken Tate

10 11 12 13 14 | Printed in China | 9 8 7 6 5 4 3 2 1

Regrets over yesterday and the fear of tomorrow are twin thieves that rob us of the moment.
—Amish Proverb

one

"I was so sure she was the one." Emma Cotton pushed her notebook aside and stifled an exasperated sigh. Getting frustrated when they were this close to finding Rose Peterson's killer would not be productive. She looked to her best friend and business partner, Kelly Grace, as if searching for more answers.

"Dakota?" Kelly asked. "Why her more than anyone else?"

Emma had no answer for that. They had only been home from Arizona for a couple of weeks, and already the urge to track down Rose's killer was weighing Emma down like bricks tied to a drowning man. Now, as they sat in Emma's home, Emma realized the trail hadn't just gone cold. It was coated in snow and ice. She heaved a sigh.

Kelly pulled the top off a muffin and took a bite, studying Emma over the glazed top. "You sound tired."

"I am," Emma agreed, eyeing the muffin and mentally calculating how many hours of yoga and running it would take to burn through all the calories. She envied Kelly's ability to eat anything she wanted and remain lithe.

"Like you're ready to give up."

She shook her head. "I knew it wasn't going to be easy, but this ..." She gestured toward the notebook where the name of their next suspect was written. "So many clues and so many dead ends."

"I don't know if I would call them dead ends," Kelly countered.

Emma tapped the eraser end of her pencil against the notepad and ran her other hand through her shoulder-length blond hair. Hannah Beiler's name was written there. Hannah Beiler, who had been enrolled in Visual Studies in Textile Design. Who had reportedly been angry with Rose shortly before she fell to her death. Who had been seen glaring at Rose and muttering under her breath. And yet Emma had her doubts. "I mean, an Amish girl? She can't be the one. Perhaps we should move on to someone else."

"Being Amish doesn't mean she couldn't be responsible," Kelly pointed out. "It could just as easily be her as anyone else in the class."

"But they're so ... religious." Emma's knowledge of the Amish was pretty thin, but she did know they were a nonviolent, God-fearing people. Murder just didn't seem likely.

"And religious people are perfect."

Emma shook her head. "I didn't say that, but there has been a plausible reason to suspect everyone else from Rose's class. But Hannah Beiler—"

"Had something against Rose."

"Rose gave her a D in her class. That's hardly grounds for murder."

"Think about it," Kelly said. "She's probably been quilting since she was big enough to hold a needle. You know what I heard? Amish women sew a mistake into every quilt so people know they're handmade. That's how perfect their stitches are. Now you tell me, if you could sew like that, would you expect a D in a quilting class?"

Emma shook her head. True, Amish quilts were something of a legend. Yet, as much as she wanted to believe the reportedly frowning and glaring Hannah Beiler was indeed a person of interest, in this case she couldn't convince herself.

"Besides, she can't be too Amish if she was taking a college class," Kelly added. "They only go to school through the eighth grade."

"How do you know so much about the Amish?" Emma caved and reached for a muffin. Instead of their usual chocolate, today's fare was orange–poppy seed. Maybe if she didn't eat the glaze frosting ….

Kelly shrugged. "Mom's ladies' group goes down to Pennsylvania to Amish country every year or two. They eat and shop. She usually brings back loads of stuff. Chocolate, apple butter, and fabric. You name it, they have it."

Kelly was right. Hannah Beiler was just as much a suspect as any of the other class members. "No stone unturned," Emma said, abandoning her muffin in favor of booting up her laptop. "OK, what was an Amish girl doing in a college class?"

"They have some sort of rites-of-passage time, where they can run around and do whatever they want before they join the church."

"For real?"

Kelly shrugged. "So I've been told. They even have a name for it. Rum-something or other. Anyway, they get to go experience the world. Maybe that's what Hannah was doing in Rose's class."

"Experiencing the world, huh?" Enough to commit murder? Is that why she seemed to have disappeared? Because she was hiding from the police? Emma shook her head. She was getting melodramatic.

"Here we go." Kelly smiled as she watched Emma begin to type.

"How do we go about finding an Amish girl?"

"I suppose the same way we search for anyone else: Google."

Emma chewed her lip as she typed Hannah's name into the search engine.

"I think it's *e-i-l*," Kelly said, although the name on the quilt was hard to read.

After seeing the list of *i-e-l*'s that popped up on the screen, Emma wasn't quite so sure. "There are hundreds." She tried not to let the disappointment creep into her voice. With each mouse click, her heart sank a little lower. There were Hannah Beilers and Hannah Bielers in Ohio, Pennsylvania, and even one in Oklahoma. "I don't know, Kelly."

"Maybe we should call the detective again."

"Tom?" Emma asked incredulously. Tom Boyer, deputy chief of the Mystic Harbor police force, was not interested in helping them solve a fifteen-year-old murder case.

"No, Alex."

Alex Manning, a private investigator, had helped them when they were in over their heads a few times. "I'm not ready to give up yet."

"I'm not saying to give up," Kelly said. "Just get some help."

Emma opened a new tab and punched in the name of Hawthorne College, where Rose had been teaching a textile design close when she died. A few short clicks later, she had a picture of Hannah Beiler, although it was fifteen years old. Emma could see the light of fire in Hannah's blue eyes. The girl wore no makeup and not particularly Amish-looking clothes, but that didn't mean much.

She flipped back to the images of the multitude of Hannah Beilers. None matched the young girl on the school website.

"She could have quit being Amish," Kelly said.

Emma shrugged. "I guess so." She continued through the photos. There was nothing, not one thing about Hannah Beiler in all the pages listed.

"What if she went back home?"

"Home?" Emma asked. "Where would that be?"

"Wherever the Amish are …. Pennsylvania? Ohio?"

Emma clicked back to the school site, opened a new tab, and … bingo. "New York," she said triumphantly.

"New York?"

"Fort Plain, to be exact. That's where she was from. If she returned to the Amish, it only makes sense that she would go back to her family and friends."

Kelly nodded. "But if she didn't …."

"We'll call Alex."

"Agreed," Kelly said. "Now, how do we know?"

"I guess there's only one way to find out."

A crash sounded from the foyer, and Emma nearly jumped out of her skin. Almost from the beginning of their investigation, it seemed as though someone had been following their every move—someone intent on stopping them. They had endured break-ins, threats, and even identity theft. The harassment had even followed them most recently to Arizona, where they had been nearly killed after being run off the road along a mountain pass. The pressure from whoever was stalking them was still fresh in her mind.

"Yoo-hoo!" Dottie Faye's voice drifted in from the front of the house.

Emma breathed a sigh of relief.

"I thought you were going to take her key," Kelly said.

Emma shot her a look.

"Right." Kelly sat back. A smile twitched at the corners of her mouth.

They both knew Dottie Faye Sinclair only did what Dottie Faye Sinclair wanted to do. Despite the fact that her unorthodox methods drove Emma crazy on a regular basis, she loved her aunt and her kooky ways.

"In the kitchen, Dottie Faye." Emma stood and pulled down a coffee mug for her aunt. The minute Dottie Faye found out they were talking about Rose's case, she would settle in for the afternoon. *Might as well embrace it.*

She had just filled the mug when Dottie Faye swept into the kitchen, her kitten heels clicking against the tile floor. She carted in two enormous sacks and hoisted them onto the table. "I bought you something."

In typical Dottie Faye fashion, she wore leopard print stretch pants and a see-through black silky blouse with matching cami underneath. More often than not these days, it seemed her aunt was channeling her inner Peg Bundy. Blond wig. Stiletto heels that amplified her height. Her multitude of bracelets clinking together reminded Emma of jingle bells in December.

"What is it?" Emma asked.

"Roman fabrics."

"Like gladiators?" Kelly frowned.

Dottie Faye *tsked.* "No. Like Antonio Roman and his fabric line. I thought it might help in your search."

Emma pressed her lips together and carefully chose her words. She didn't want to hurt her aunt's feelings. "How exactly is looking at his fabrics going to help us solve this case?"

"We've already cleared him as a suspect," Kelly added.

The DNA tests had come back negative, clearing the fabric genius. In fact, when Rose's former student found out what they were trying to do, he had offered his assistance.

Dottie Faye shrugged her slim shoulders, hurt easing across her perfectly made-up features. "If you don't want it ...."

"No, no. That's not it." Emma shook her head. "Who

wouldn't want Antonio Roman's fabric? He's amazing."

"Definitely. Thank you so much, Dottie Faye."

Dottie Faye's puckered frown turned into a beaming smile. "It's beautiful stuff, really." She started unloading the rich fabric, stacking the thick cuts one on top of the other. "Any word on that Amish girl?"

Emma shook her head. "We know she was from Fort Plain, New York. She probably returned there after college."

Dottie Faye finished stacking the fabrics. "You know what I think? I think you should just get in the car and drive over there and see her."

Kelly pulled the laptop toward her and clicked some keys. "That's almost a four-hour drive. Plus, we don't know if she's even there."

"Only one way to find out." Dottie Faye eyed them both over the rim of her coffee mug as she took a generous sip. "Unless you'd rather fly."

Emma automatically shook her head. She had done a great many things for this case, but she'd spend four hours in a car before spending one in an airplane. Hadn't the trips first to England and then out to Arizona been enough?

"Even if she's not there, maybe we can find someone in her family who knows where she is," Kelly said.

Emma had to agree. "Plus we need a DNA sample to send to the lab." In order to get a DNA sample, they needed to meet Hannah.

"That's settled then." Dottie Faye rubbed her hands together expectantly. "When do we leave?"

"We?" Emma and Kelly echoed in unison.

"Of course. I told you from the beginning that I wanted to help. We can take my car."

As Dottie Faye prattled on about maps and gas mileage,

Emma knew two things: They were on their way upstate, and they needed a crash course in all things Amish.

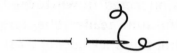

"OK." Dottie Faye looked from Emma to Kelly and back again. Emma had the strangest feeling of being back in school. "Here are some handouts I gathered."

Handouts? Spy cams and voice-activated digital recorders Emma could understand. But handouts? She felt like she was at an FBI briefing.

Kelly shot Emma a look, but took the paper that Dottie Faye thrust her way.

"Now, the Amish," Dottie Faye said, "are also called 'Plain People.' They are very religious and don't use electricity. They don't even have telephones—of any sort—except for ones on the side of the road."

"Uh-hum, Dottie Faye, we know all of this."

Dottie Faye nodded sagely. "They don't have a lot to do with the English—that's what they call non-Amish folks—though sometimes they live in houses right next door to each other. Ain't that something?"

Emma and Kelly nodded obligingly.

"Now, here's a picture of an Amish man and woman." She thrust an 8 x 10 glossy at them. "They all dress alike, but they don't allow people to take their pictures." She turned the photo around to study it more closely. "Though I don't know how they got this picture if they don't let people photograph them." She shrugged as if chalking it up to one of the mysteries of the world and continued her monologue on the Amish. "They ride around in horse-drawn buggies, and not one of them owns a car."

"Yes, we know," Kelly said. Emma had to hand it to her: Kelly managed to keep the exasperation out of her tone.

"Since they're so secretive and closed, I figure we won't be able to just walk up to one of them and start asking a lot of questions, so I booked us a couple of rooms at the Yoder Bed and Breakfast there in Fort Plain. We can act like tourists, and no one will ever be the wiser." She clapped her hands in excitement.

"That sounds great, Dottie Faye."

"We have the rooms for two weeks. That should give us plenty of time to track down this Hannah person. Now, I'll take my new Dottie cam. I bet I could get some good video there."

"New one?" Kelly asked. Oh, she just had to ask.

"Oh, it's the neatest thing—see? It looks like a regular ol' brooch. And you just pin it to your—"

But she stopped as Emma shook her head. "I don't think that's such a good idea. I mean, if they don't like to have their pictures taken, I'm sure they don't allow video either."

Dottie Faye *pshawed*. "They aren't going to *know* I'm filming them. That's the whole point of having it hidden in a flower."

Emma glanced at Kelly, who shook her head.

"We'll check into the B&B and start asking questions," Emma said.

"Who knows?" Kelly added. "She may have even gotten married."

"True." A lot could happen in fifteen years.

"And that could be exactly why we can't find anything about her online," Kelly said. "Well, that and the fact that she's Amish." She took her last bite of muffin. "Do we have any contacts in New York?"

Emma shook her head.

"I have a friend there," Dottie Faye chimed in. "Of course, she lives in the city."

"I meant upstate New York, Dottie Faye." Kelly reached for another muffin.

How she can eat so much and stay so thin is a mystery for the ages. Emma looked to her own half-eaten snack, envying her friend.

Dottie Faye shrugged. "I suppose not." Then her eyes lit up, and a smile danced across her face. "Do you think we should go undercover? We could all dress like the Amish and wear those little cap thingies like they do."

"That means no makeup."

Dottie Faye's smile fell. "Never mind," she said.

Emma bit her lip, suppressing a laugh. Dottie Faye wouldn't be caught outside the house without lipstick perfectly in place. Not even in Amish country.

But the laughter stilled in her throat as a crash sounded at the front of the cottage.

They all raced into the foyer as tires screeched outside. A brick lay in the shattered glass of the front window, the sheer curtains blowing in the afternoon breeze.

Kelly ran to the window. "Darn it, they're already gone."

"Did you see the car at all?" Emma asked.

She shook her head. "I couldn't even tell the color."

"Girls." Dottie Faye pointed to the brick that had been tossed through Emma's window. "There's a note attached."

They stood in a semicircle around the brick, each one looking at the other.

"Should we pick it up?" Emma asked.

Dottie Faye shook her head. "You'll ruin the fingerprints."

"Can you lift fingerprints from paper?" Kelly asked.

"I would think so." Emma took a deep breath, willing her heart back to its rightful place in her chest. This whole stalker situation was getting out of hand. "If not, maybe from the brick."

"Are you going to call the police?" Kelly asked as Emma continued to eye the brick as if it were a snake about to strike.

"If you don't call the police, you won't be able to claim the damage to the window on your insurance," Dottie Faye pointed out.

The police would be no help, and they all knew it. By the time Emma calculated her deductible, she might as well just pay for the repairs out of pocket.

"I'm not calling the police. I'm going to read the note and carefully put it away in case we need it later. Agreed?"

"Later for what?" Dottie Faye asked.

"Agreed?" Emma repeated.

"Agreed," Kelly echoed.

Emma turned to look at Dottie Faye.

"Oh," she huffed. "Agreed. Though I still think you should call that handsome detective."

Emma resisted the urge to roll her eyes. "Just think. If I cut my hand, I can call the good doctor." Her aunt was constantly trying to set Emma up with Dr. Eric Hart—a "true Southern gentleman," as Dottie Faye called him.

"We should call him anyway," Dottie Faye said. "That scare might be giving me the vapors."

Emma picked her way through the broken glass. Perhaps they should have swept up first.

"Be careful," Kelly said as Emma used her napkin to carefully pick up the brick and shook the glass off.

She backed away until she was standing on clean floor once again.

Her heart raced in her chest as she removed the rubber band from the brick and let it fall to the floor. She set the brick on the small table near the door. Her hands trembled as she carefully unfolded the paper. She hoped that if there were fingerprints on it, she wasn't destroying a good clue.

"Leave well enough alone or else!"

"Or else *what?*" Kelly asked.

"I don't know," Emma whispered, "but it can't be good."

two

Emma wasn't about to let something like a broken window and a threatening note scare her away. They didn't even know for sure that the person responsible for Rose's death was also to blame for all of the threats and attacks on them.

Who was she trying to kid? Of course he—or she—was.

Maybe getting away to Amish New York would give whoever was harassing them time to settle down. Perhaps it'd be safer there. After all, what could happen in a quaint Amish community?

Dottie Faye slammed the trunk of the Caddy closed and came around to the driver's seat. "Y'all ready to go?"

Emma and Kelly nodded as Dottie Faye slid behind the wheel and started the engine.

"Here." Dottie Faye handed Emma a folded map. "You get to navigate."

Emma stared at the map. "Why don't we use GPS?"

Dottie Faye gasped. "Where's the fun in that?" She put the car in reverse and backed out of the drive. "Also, I didn't like the way the Yankee in that little box kept bossing me around. I threw him out the window."

Five hours in the car with Dottie Faye and a paper map. Heaven help them all.

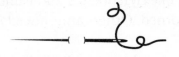

Amish country in New York looked like something out of a travel brochure—rolling green hills dotted with sheep and cattle, huge red barns with tarnished weather vanes, and aged fence posts strung with rusted barbed wire. Emma felt as if she had driven into another world.

What had it been like for Hannah Beiler to grow up here? Why would she ever want to leave?

"The B&B is on the far side of town," said Dottie Faye. "We should be able to check in and get right to work."

"Dottie Faye," Emma said, "we will have to proceed with … diplomacy. Do you know what I mean?"

Dottie Faye waved a hand in her direction. "Of course, sugar. I can be diplomatic when the situation calls for it. Blending in, that's my forté."

Well, Emma wouldn't exactly call it *that*. She surreptitiously eyed today's ensemble. Her aunt wore a bright green outfit that looked like it belonged at a roller derby from the seventies. The white button-down she wore over it toned it down a bit, but any conservatism she gained from the menswear-inspired shirt was lost in the high-heeled purple pumps and matching fedora. They were going to stick out like space aliens at the county fair.

But she loved Dottie Faye and decided not to counter her statement. "Let's just check in and then go from there."

"Perfect," Kelly chimed in.

The town of Fort Plain was a strange mixture of new and old. The buildings themselves seemed frozen in time except for the new franchises that looked strangely out of place. The stores had names like Hershberger and Lambright, their signs simple and unadorned. Others announced Amish goods and food for sale.

"It's bigger than I thought." Kelly leaned forward in her

seat to get a better look at the quaint little town.

"Charming," Dottie Faye murmured as she slowed to a stop at the traffic light.

Cars and trucks of all sorts shared the road with scooters and horse-drawn buggies with distinctive brown tops.

"I wonder if there's a quilt shop," Kelly mused.

"Oh, I'm sure," Emma said, half-turning in her seat. "Look there." She pointed to the large sign that read Yoder Mercantile.

"Yoder," Kelly said. "Do you think that's the same family as the B&B?"

Emma shrugged. "How many Yoders could there be?"

"There's about twelve hundred Amish here," Dottie Faye said. "I read that on the Internet. You'd know that too if you'd bothered to read my handout. Page three." She sniffed. "Didn't check on how many fancy folk."

"'Fancy folk'?" Emma asked.

"Well, if the Amish are Plain folk, then everyone else must be fancy."

They rolled through the town, finally pulling into a small parking space next to the Yoder B&B.

The renovated house, white clapboard with trellises up each side, looked like something out of an old black-and-white movie. The wide porch stretched across the front, then disappeared around each side. Wicker rockers dotted the planked porch and welcomed visitors to sit a spell. Pots of bright red geraniums and deep purple pansies added much-needed color.

"Delightful," Kelly said as Emma pulled their suitcases from the trunk. She stretched the kinks out of her back and studied the house. It was from another time. A place such as this made atrocities like murder seem a million miles away.

"It is something." Dottie Faye pulled her sunglasses back into place with a decisive *click*.

"Are you filming this?" Emma asked in a hushed whisper. Behind Dottie Faye, a horse pulling a buggy clopped down the street, a car inching slowly along behind.

Dottie Faye turned in a complete circle. "Just to get a feel for the place. I didn't think you wanted me to bring my flower cam."

"That didn't mean I wanted you to bring your sunglasses."

"Oh, pooh," Dottie Faye said and kept right on filming.

"Does that mean you didn't bring your brooch Dottie cam?" Kelly asked.

"Of course I didn't." Dottie Faye waved away the silly thought with an expressive flick of her hand.

"I didn't think so," Emma said under her breath, and she started up the steps.

"Once we get checked in, we can start looking around. Maybe walk down to the mercantile and see what we can find out." Dottie Faye, it seemed, was in full Sherlock Holmes mode.

Emma shook her head at her aunt's gung-ho attitude and stepped into the Yoder B&B.

Not surprisingly, the foyer was as quaint as the outside. Slick green potted plants accented the pale blue paint and rich dark wood. A small, chest-high desk sat just inside the door; an old-fashioned registry book and an ink pen shaped like a quill anticipated incoming guests. The combined scents of lemon furniture polish and cinnamon wafted around them.

An impressive staircase sat to the left, sweeping up to the second floor and beyond. To the right, an open parlor invited with soft-looking chairs and bright windows. Just beyond the foyer, Emma could make out a large dining table that looked as if it could seat her entire quilting club, the Nimble Thimbles, from back home in Mystic Harbor.

"May I help you?" A sophisticated brunette appeared from the room around the corner, the scent of expensive perfume mixing with the ambiance of the inn. She was the last type of person Emma would have expected to be running the Yoder B&B. She was polished and poised, in perfectly pressed slacks and a flowing silk blouse. An elegant strand of pearls encircled her neck, and diamonds flashed at her ears. Emma guessed her age to be late fifties, though she carried it with grace.

Dottie Faye hesitated a moment. Maybe she didn't know what to make of such a non-Amish worker in the B&B either. Then she pushed her sunglasses to the top of her head. Somehow she managed the action without rumpling one strand of her perfectly coiffed blond hair.

"Sinclair." She stepped forward, using her gracious upbringing to her advantage. That was Dottie Faye. She could turn on her Southern charm whenever she needed. The chic and stylish woman behind the counter had nothing on Dottie Faye when she set her mind to it. "We have a reservation for a suite."

"Sylvia Yoder. So happy to have you here." The woman smiled and ran one perfectly manicured nail down the reservations book. "Sinclair. Here we are." She opened the shallow cabinet behind the small podium desk and found the keys. "Room 3B. There are two suites on the third floor. Yours is the one on the left."

"Thank you." Dottie Faye took the keys and pocketed them before either Emma or Kelly could protest.

"Breakfast is served between six and eight. Tea is at four. There are a few great places to eat, but the diner is the closest. A lot of our guests like to walk down there for lunch and dinner." She retrieved a few pamphlets from inside the desk and handed one to each of them. "The Mennonites who run the Amish store have a tour that goes throughout the day. You can ride in a horse-drawn wagon through the Amish community. It's great fun, if you're so inclined." She stopped with a smile. "Do you have any questions?"

"Is there someone to help with our bags?" Dottie Faye asked.

"Dottie Faye!" Emma shook her head at her aunt's antics. Emma knew she considered any physical labor to be "man's work," but for a minute she had been hopeful that her aunt might just behave herself this trip. She should have known better.

"My son can help with your bags." She rang the bell near the registration book, and a young man appeared. He was tall and lean, towering over all of them as he shifted uncomfortably in his sneakers. "Rusty, can you help our guests to their suite? It's 3B," she added.

"Sure." Somehow he managed to gather up all of their suitcases, leaving them to carry only their own overnight bags. Not a bad deal considering they had to climb two flights of stairs.

"I hope you can make it to four o'clock tea today," Sylvia said in parting. "It's always nice for the guests to get together."

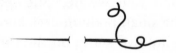

"Tea?" Dottie Faye asked as they shut the door to their suite. "Is that Amish?"

Kelly shook her head. "I don't think so."

"Well, I want the Amish experience," Dottie Faye harrumphed.

"I'm sure we can find someone who will let you help them can tomatoes and milk the cows." Emma smiled in response to the horrified look on her aunt's face.

"Ugh!" Dottie Faye held up her hands as if to stave off the unspeakable. "That is *not* what I meant."

Emma turned in a circle, examining the room from all angles. Like the town and the B&B itself, the room was beautifully sweet. Simple and sturdy, the furniture appeared comfortable and serviceable. Farmland prints in plain wood frames dotted the pale aqua walls. There was a small living area and a shared bathroom to go with the two bedrooms.

"The couch makes out into a bed," Dottie Faye said. "I figure we can take turns sleeping in here. That way one of us will always be on watch."

"I don't think that's necessary," Kelly said. "But I'll sleep out here."

Dottie Faye picked up the framed list of available channels next to the television set. "No, sugar, I'll take the couch."

"Home Shopping Network?" Emma asked.

Dottie Faye beamed. "Don't you know it."

Kelly laughed and grabbed her suitcase. "Which bedroom you want, Emma?"

"I don't think it matters."

Her friend nodded and dragged her cases into the room farthest from the door. Dottie Faye started unpacking her clothes into what appeared to be some kind of coat closet. That left Emma to cart her own bags into the second bedroom.

It was everything she had expected and more. Though it seemed a little fancy for Amish standards, Emma was certain the allure of staying at an Amish B&B had more to do with proximity to the community and fantastic—albeit fattening—food the Amish were known for.

The walls were the same pale aqua as the sitting area, and again the furniture looked aged and reliable. There was a queen-size bed, a highboy dresser, and a rich wood rocking chair. Pictures of farmland and flowers decorated the walls, all understated in order to bow to the room's showpiece. A gorgeous handmade quilt graced the bed. The colors were bold—reds, yellows, and oranges mixed with just a touch of lime green and backed with an immaculate black. The design was wild yet meticulous. Could it be Amish sewn? It only made sense. But she couldn't wrap her mind around the plain, simple-loving Amish and the incredible quilt before her.

Suitcase forgotten, she ran her fingers along the top of the bed. *Beautiful* wasn't the word for such a quilt. *Exquisite* and *inspiring*—those fit better.

The business side of her stirred to life. With quilts like this in the shop, they would have visitors from all over.

She made a mental note to ask Sylvia about the quilt. In fact, she had quite a few questions to ask their hostess. Like, where could a person purchase such a quilt? Was she the Yoder in the B&B's name? Did she know anyone named Hannah Beiler?

Kelly lightly rapped on the open door and sauntered into the room. "I see you got one too," she said, nodding toward the quilt.

"It's something, isn't it?"

"They're unlike any quilts I've ever seen, Amish or not."

"I wonder if we could get a couple for the shop."

"To display or sell?" Kelly asked.

"Maybe both. I mean, we have only antique quilts, but these are spectacular."

"We can ask Sylvia."

"I was just thinking about that," Emma said, "wondering how we should approach her. I get this feeling—"

"Like the more we talk to people, the more they're going to withhold."

"Exactly." Emma sighed. "Why is that?"

"I dunno."

Kelly eased onto the bed as Emma unpacked her suitcase. She had tried to bring understated clothing. They had taken a little bit of time to research the Amish before they left Mystic Harbor, but the more they learned, the more they realized that for a reportedly simple people, the Amish were strangely complex. There were Amish who rode bicycles and those who didn't. Some had cellphones, while others weren't allowed to use them at all.

But for each, one thing was the same. They dressed in plain clothing and covered their hair most of the time.

Emma refolded her gray sweater, then smoothed her hands down her jeans. Regardless of the lack of color in their clothes, the trio would stick out as tourists. She could only hope the community was receptive to the questions they were going to ask.

"Do you really think she's here?" Kelly asked as she examined the quilt. Her voice sounded offhanded and casual, but Emma knew better. They had been through so much to get where they were today.

"It makes sense, doesn't it? If this was where she was from, and she returned here, she'd surely be here. I hope."

"What if she's not? What do we do then?"

Emma shrugged and pushed the suitcase under the bed for storage. "Then we pick another name from the student list that we haven't talked to and go find them."

"As much as I don't believe that Hannah Beiler is our killer, I still hope she is."

The search seemed to be taking its toll on Kelly. It was taking a toll on them all.

"I know what you mean," Emma said. "And there's only one way to find out."

"Find Hannah."

Emma nodded. "And get a DNA sample."

It sounded simple enough, but as the case had taught them, sounding easy and being easy were two very different things.

"All right, chickadees." Dottie Faye poked her head into Emma's room. Her sunglasses were still perched on her nose, no doubt filming away. "Who's ready for tea?"

"I'm always ready for a snack." Kelly stood and smoothed the wrinkles from the quilt.

Emma shook her head with a smile. "You know, if enough of the other guests are there too, this might be a good time to find out more about the community."

"I can eat and investigate," Kelly said.

"Is that what you're wearing?" Emma nodded toward Dottie Faye in her bright pink pants and leopard print top.

Dottie Faye looked down at herself. "Something wrong?"

"I thought the plan was to try and blend in as much as possible. We don't want to look too much like tourists."

"Sugar, the minute I open my mouth, they're going to know I don't belong here."

True enough. "Just—"

"Keep it on the DL," Dottie Faye said. "I know." And with that she turned on one spiky heel and started for the door.

"DL?" Emma mouthed at Kelly.

"The down-low," Kelly muttered in return.

Leave it to Kelly to have all the hip answers. Emma guessed that having teenagers did have its occasional advantages.

Though she was certain that Dottie Faye had never kept anything on the down-low her entire life.

three

Tea was just as Emma imagined. Silver trays of cookies and other homemade treats tempted her from all around the dining room. Kelly and Dottie Faye piled their tiny saucers high, but Emma refrained, calculating calories and reminding herself of the richness of Amish food—even if it was only Amish inspired.

The guests at the B&B milled around, using the time to refuel as well as socialize. An older couple sat on the overlarge armchair, their snowy heads nearly touching as they talked to each other. A pair of twenty-something girls occupied the small bistro table, giggling over the glossy magazine between them.

Emma, Kelly, and Dottie Faye claimed the couch as their spot, setting their coffee cups on the low table in front of them.

"I'm so glad they had coffee." Dottie Faye smiled over her plate of cookies. "Who should we talk to first?" she said in a low whisper. "I'm thinking him." She nodded toward a big man in a cowboy hat.

"He's definitely a tourist, and he doesn't look like he'd know anything," Kelly said, glancing around the room.

"Maybe that's what he *wants* you to think."

Emma hid her smile behind her coffee cup and gave the room her own perusal. They were all tourists. Not one person in the room looked to know any more about the Amish than she did. "I say we finish our snacks then head down to the mercantile. If Hannah Beiler has returned to Fort Plain, she probably shops in there."

"Good idea." Kelly nodded.

"I've got fresh buttermilk cookies, if anyone would like one," an Amish girl called from the doorway. She carried in a small platter piled high with fabulous-smelling cookies.

"I would love one." Emma stood and waved the girl to her.

With a shy smile, she approached. Emma guessed she was around fifteen or sixteen, though her fresh-scrubbed, innocent face made it hard to pinpoint her age exactly. She probably hadn't even been alive when Rose was killed, but that didn't mean she wouldn't know Hannah Beiler.

"Thank you," Emma said, taking a cookie.

The girl gave a tiny dip of a bow then offered the plate to Kelly and Dottie Faye. "Would you like one?"

They each accepted a cookie as Emma cautiously nibbled hers. It crumbled in her mouth like a scone, the flavor an unbelievable mix of sweet vanilla with crunchy walnuts.

Kelly swallowed. "Is this an Amish recipe?"

"*Jah.* I mean, yes."

"And you are—" Emma asked, her heart beating just a little faster.

"Amish, *jah.*"

Perfect.

"You wouldn't happen to know Hannah Beiler?" Dottie Faye blurted.

The young girl blinked.

"What my aunt means is we are looking for a woman named Hannah Beiler."

"Is she a friend of yours?" The girl's accent sounded like a mix of German and something else Emma couldn't place.

"Something like that," Kelly said evasively.

"I'm Emma Cotton. This is my aunt Dottie Faye Sinclair and my friend Kelly Grace."

"How do you do? I'm Casey Yoder."

"Yoder?" Kelly asked. "Like the name on the front?"

"Sort of. The woman who owns this bed-and-breakfast is my *aenti*—my aunt," she explained.

Emma frowned. "But she doesn't dress like you." She nodded toward the girl's plain burgundy dress and black apron. Her honey-blond hair was pulled back at the nape of her neck, the sides twisted slightly before disappearing under the little linen cap pinned to her head.

"*Nay*, she has turned English."

"Is that easy to do, turn English?" Kelly asked.

"Casey?" The girl was kept from answering by the sound of her aunt's voice. "You have cookies piling up in the kitchen."

She gave them an apologetic twist of her mouth that was almost a smile. "I must go."

"Wait," Emma said, laying a hand on the girl's arm. "Can we talk to you again?"

"I suppose." A small frown wrinkled her brow. "But why do you want to talk to me?"

"We came a long way to visit our friend. It seems like you can help us with that."

"Casey?" Mrs. Yoder called again.

"Coming, *Aenti*," she called then lowered her voice for only the three of them to hear. "I get off work at six. I can talk to you then."

Jackpot! "That would be fine. Should we meet you right here?"

Casey shook her head. "I'll meet you at the diner."

"Six o'clock it is," Kelly said before Casey scurried away.

"That was strange," Dottie Faye said as she watched the girl's retreating back.

"It was," Emma agreed.

"Do you think she knows something?" Kelly asked.

"I know she does." Dottie Faye gave a confident nod.

But Emma shook her head. "I don't think so, at least nothing bad."

Kelly agreed. "But if she can lead us to Hannah Beiler ...."

"I've been thinking about something: What if Hannah's married? She wouldn't be Hannah Beiler any longer." She had a feeling there wouldn't be any modern-day hyphenating of names here in Fort Plain.

"I thought of that. But if we find a Beiler family, surely they would help us find Hannah, whatever her name is now."

"I hope so." Emma sighed wistfully, then took one last bite of her cookie. "Let's go over to the mercantile while we wait. Maybe someone over there knows something."

They put their cups and saucers on the sideboard and ran upstairs to grab their purses. Being on the third floor had its advantages. With enough trips up to their room, Emma wouldn't have to worry about trivial things such as calories and fat grams in buttermilk cookies.

"Should we drive?" Dottie Faye jangled her keys, but Emma shook her head.

"It's such a nice day; let's walk."

She looked ready to protest when Kelly linked their arms. "Come on, Dottie Faye, the walk will do us good."

The streets of the small town were lined with shops of all sorts, from a fancy boutique to an Amish market. From where Emma was standing, it looked more like it was for tourists than the Amish themselves.

Carriages pulled by beautiful horses were parked next to cars of all makes and models. The past and present seemed blended together.

"We have to go in there," Kelly said, pointing to a shop called Needles & Notions. A beautiful quilt that looked like green fire on a navy blue background lay over an antique steamer trunk in the window.

Emma's feet stopped automatically, her love for all things quilted battling with her obligations to Rose. "We'll come back," she said.

"It'll have to be tomorrow," Kelly added. "They close at six."

Dottie Faye pushed her glasses onto the top of her head and peered into the window. Never one to sew more than a button on in an emergency, Dottie Faye would rather be staked on an ant hill and covered in honey than spend the afternoon browsing for fabrics.

Emma shook her head at the myriad of differences between herself and her aunt.

"And we have to meet Casey," Dottie Faye said, no doubt searching for a reason not to enter the quaint little store.

"But definitely before we leave," Emma promised.

"While y'all do that, I think I'll go check out what's happening in there." Dottie Faye pointed across the street at the plate glass windows of the Fort Plain Gym for Men.

"Aunt Dottie." In her exasperation, Emma forgot to call her aunt by her given name and received a frown for her lapse. "Dottie Faye," she corrected. "There'll be no matchmaking this trip."

"I was talking about for me." She grinned. "But since you brought it up, I'll be on my best behavior. You need to save your love for the good doctor." She turned and started up the street in front of them.

Emma shook her head as Kelly clamped a hand over her mouth to stem her laughter.

"It's not funny."

"It is from where I'm standing."

OK, so Emma had a *tiny* thing for the man. But it had never gone anywhere. Well, nowhere significant. Sure, he and his adorable daughter had spent Easter with her crazy bunch at Kelly's. If that hadn't run the man off, as Dottie Faye would say, Emma supposed nothing would. But still she wondered if all he wanted from her was friendship because he was still grieving for his wife.

Dottie Faye turned back to them. "Are you coming or not?"

Emma joined arms with Kelly, and together they marched behind Dottie Faye all the way to the Yoder Mercantile.

The first thing Emma noticed was that the mercantile had no electricity, and the second was that they were the only non-Amish folk inside.

"It's OK that we're in here, right?" Kelly said from the corner of her mouth.

"I hope so," Emma replied.

Dottie Faye's chin rose to a defiant angle that said she was staying regardless.

This should be interesting.

"*Goedemiddag.*" The shop owner smiled and nodded in their direction, the sunlight from the windows glinting off his plain round glasses.

"That sounded like a greeting, not 'get out,'" Emma said. "So I guess we're OK."

Emma grabbed Dottie Faye's elbow before she could march herself up to the counter. "Play it cool, please. We don't want to scare anyone off."

"Gotcha."

She loved her aunt, she really did. She knew Dottie Faye meant well, but there were times ....

Dottie Faye stuck out one shoulder and turned slowly from side to side as if sweeping the room.

She had an oversized Dottie Cam brooch pinned to her shirt.

"Are you recording this?" Emma whispered.

"Of course."

"Just keep it on the down-low."

"Honey, I got this." Dottie Faye smiled her Southern beauty queen smile and started wandering the aisles, her brooch leading the way.

"Can I help you?" The man behind the counter approached. He wore a white butcher's apron over black pants and a sky blue shirt. His beard was long and a bit on the scraggly side with no moustache.

"Hi, we're up for the weekend," Kelly started.

"Or longer," Emma added.

"*Ach, gut, gut,*" the man said in an accent much like Casey Yoder's.

"We're staying at the Yoder B&B," Kelly continued.

"Is the owner a relative of yours?" Emma tried to sound like she was just making polite conversation and not grilling him for information.

"*Jah*, she is my *shveshtah*—my sister."

"You're not Casey's dad?"

"So you have met little Casey." He shook his head. "I am her uncle."

Emma let her gaze stray across the store, quickly noting where her aunt was and what she was doing. So far, so good. Dottie Faye was in the corner, studying the contents of the thick bookcase there. Or at least pretending to.

"Your store is very interesting." Emma said, searching for a lead-in to her questions. "You don't have electricity?"

"*Nay*, our *Ordnung* does not allow electricity."

"Not even for commercial use?" Kelly asked.

The man looked a little confused.

"You aren't even allowed to use it in the store?"

"There is no need. We open when the sun comes up, and we close when it goes down."

"We came up here to look for our friend," Emma said. "Hannah Beiler."

Recognition flashed in his blue eyes, but the man's expression changed, then closed off. It was as if he had mentally shut them out. "There are plenty of Hannah Beilers in the district, but none that I know with *Englisch frenden*." He said the last two words as if they were a communicable disease.

"Abner," a woman in a black bonnet, dressed much the same as young Casey, called to the storeowner from the front counter.

"I will be there in a minute, Gracie Chupp." He turned back to Emma and Kelly. "I must go see to my other customers. Let me know if there is something else you need."

I need Hannah Beiler, Emma wanted to shout, but she knew that she would have to bide her time if she wanted to learn something from such a tightly knit people. If all the Amish had the same reaction as Abner Yoder, it was going to take a while.

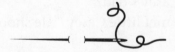

"Did you see the book section in there?" Dottie Faye asked as they exited the store into the waning daylight. Another couple of hours and it would be completely dark. Their first day in Fort Plain and no clues to be found. "Not one magazine in sight."

"Your magazines will be waiting when we return home," Emma assured her.

"There it is." Kelly pointed toward the end of the street.

The Amish Dinner Bell was the name on the outside. Considering the lights blazing inside the restaurant, Emma was fairly certain no practicing Amish actually owned the diner—at least according to what they had learned from the shopkeeper about electricity.

It was almost the dinner hour, and the place was starting to get busy. But they had no trouble locating Casey Yoder in a corner booth.

"Thanks for meeting us," Emma said after everyone had gotten settled. The young and harried-looking waitress hustled around the counter, handed out menus, promised waters all around, and then disappeared into the kitchen.

"So you think you might know Hannah Beiler?"

"*Jah*," Casey nodded and took a sip of the drink she had ordered before their arrival. "Well, I know three Hannah Beilers."

Emma's heart fell. But three was good, right?

"One is my cousin who is three, so I'm pretty sure she's not who you are looking for."

"And the other two?" Kelly asked.

Dottie Faye pulled her sunglasses back into place and scanned the room, no doubt filming for future use.

"One is a friend of mine, and the other is a *gros gross-mammi*. How do you say? Great-grandmother?"

"I was so hoping you knew our friend Hannah Beiler." Emma tried to keep the disappointment from her voice.

"*Ach*, but I do," she said sounding so much like her uncle. "But the woman I am thinking of isn't Hannah Beiler now. She is Hannah Lapp."

And how many of those could there be in Fort Plain? A dozen?

Casey dropped her voice so that only they could hear. "I hear my *maam* and *dat* talking once about a distant cousin of mine. They said she went out into the *Englisch* world and stayed a long time."

"And her name was Hannah Beiler?" Hope rose again in Emma's chest. Now they were getting somewhere.

"*Jah*, she was Hannah Beiler until she married Alvin Lapp."

"Did your folks say if she went off to school?" Dottie Faye pulled her sunglasses toward the tip of her nose. "Or took a quilting class at a college?"

Kelly shot Dottie Faye a look, but fortunately, Emma's aunt didn't say anything more. Kelly understood Dottie Faye's need to help, even if her efforts weren't actually very helpful.

"*Nay*. They would never admit such sins. It is too ... embarrassing."

"Sins?" Dottie Faye asked.

Casey nodded. "Amish believe that an education like that is a prideful thing, and pride is—"

"A sin," Dottie Faye finished. "Got it."

Education was a sin and going to college was an embarrassment. Emma resisted the urge to laugh ... or cry. She wasn't sure exactly which one was more fitting.

"But I thought an Amish teen could do whatever they wanted on their rumps—rumpspringey—" Emma faltered.

"*Rumspringa*," Casey corrected. "And they can, as long as their family allows the behavior. But," she said in a lowered voice, "Hannah had already joined the church."

Well, that puts a different spin on things. "Do you know how we can get in touch with Hannah Beiler ... er, Lapp?" Emma asked.

"I s'pose you'll have to drive out to her farm," Casey said. "It's a ways out of town. I would take you there, but ..." She trailed off, leaving Emma to wonder what would have finished the sentence. She had a feeling Casey didn't want anyone to know she had been talking to the strangers who had just rolled into town. If education was a bad thing, what kind of sin would fraternizing with the English be?

"Will you tell us how to get there?" Kelly asked.

"*Jah.*"

And just like that, they had their first lead.

"Perfect." Emma sighed. Finally they were getting somewhere.

four

Emma filled her plate at the breakfast buffet, bypassing the muffins in favor of dry toast with a side of fresh fruit. She wasn't sure how she could eat this morning; her stomach was in knots. Today they just might meet Rose's killer.

That same anticipation had caused her to toss and turn long into the night. She wanted to blame her sleeplessness on being in a strange room, in a strange bed, but it was dreams of Rose that kept her restless. At least now they had something to go on.

"We need a plan," Dottie Faye said once they all had their plates and were seated at the end of the long dining table.

"You're right," Kelly agreed.

Dottie Faye swallowed a bite of scrambled eggs and pointed her fork toward the big man in the cowboy hat. "I still say he's a decoy."

"Auntie," Emma started.

"Well, he could be," Dottie Faye defended, for once not correcting Emma's slip-up. "Leave no stone unturned. That's what I say."

Emma was about to protest further when Kelly jumped back into the conversation. "You know, she has a point. We're here no more than two weeks. And in that time, we have to get as much information as we can. It might be a good idea to split up in order to cover more ground."

"You know, you just might be on to something." Emma turned to her aunt. "Why don't you stay and see what sort of information you can get out of him while Kelly and I drive out to the Lapp farm?" She felt a twinge of guilt at leaving her aunt behind, but she had a feeling they would be able learn more from the conservative Amish without Dottie Faye's distraction. Not that her electric-blue hot pants and black silk leggings could be called distracting.

"Do you mean that?" Dottie Faye's face lit with excitement, and Emma's guilt deepened. She knew her aunt meant well, but this was one time Emma was certain Dottie Faye's over-the-top ways would hurt more than help.

"Sure." She shrugged as if it were no big deal. "You think you can handle it?"

Dottie Faye patted her gigantic handbag. "I'm on it," she said, beaming.

Emma said a short prayer for the man in the cowboy hat.

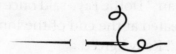

Driving through the back roads of the Amish district was both peaceful and stimulating.

"How are we going to get the DNA sample?" Kelly asked from the driver's seat.

Emma turned away from the green pasture outside the window and shrugged. "I'm not sure. Maybe we can get her to invite us in and offer us something to eat. Then we'll distract her and take her coffee cup or something."

"That is not going to work."

Emma wanted to dispute her friend's claim, but unfortunately, Kelly was probably right. The Amish were nothing if not protective of one another. And how were they going to convince Hannah to let them in the house? "All we can do is try."

Kelly shook her head. "This is going to end badly."

"Don't be so negative. We've managed this far, haven't we?"

"I suppose."

Emma sat up a little straighter in her seat, pointing to a sign up ahead. It was white with black letters, crudely painted and nailed to a fence post. All the telephone poles and electric wires had ended long ago. "Is that it?"

Kelly slowed the car as she read the hand-painted sign aloud. "'Tomatoes, jam, hickory logs.' Yep, this is the turn."

A quarter mile more and they would be at the Lapp farm. Emma just hoped they had the right girl.

"Have faith," Kelly chirped as she navigated the winding country road. Any other time, Emma would have enjoyed the beautiful scenery and the peacefulness that surrounded them, but today she was more concerned about the case.

"I think this is it," Kelly said, gently pulling the car into the narrow dirt drive. She navigated the car close to the house, parking it next to a large tree. Chickens and ducks pecked in the front yard, chasing down bugs in the sparse grass.

"Are you sure this is the right place?" Emma asked.

Sad was too kind a word for the farm. The house needed painting, badly. An old-fashioned wringer washer sat on the front porch next to a woodstove. Neither looked like they'd been used in years. Were it not for the fowl and the pen of goats on the other side of the tree, Emma would have thought the house was abandoned. There was no welcoming wreath on the door, no curtains in the windows.

"This is where Casey said." Emma turned back to the mailbox. "Lapp" was painted on the side in fading green letters.

It looked so different from the other farms they had passed. Whereas they had been clean and neat, this one just looked neglected.

Emma ran her hands down the sides of her jeans. She had worn her most boring gray T-shirt and no jewelry in order to blend in a bit more. Not that it helped. Even with her hair pulled back in a knot at her nape, she was glaringly not Amish.

She studied the house, but no one stirred. She had hoped their car would raise the suspicion of Hannah Beiler or whoever was in the house, and someone would come to investigate. No such luck. She took a deep breath and steeled herself for the worst. "Let's do this."

Kelly nodded in agreement, and Emma led the way onto the porch. The wooden planks, flat and worn, creaked and moaned with each step she took. With a quick prayer that they were on the right track, she raised her hand and knocked.

The unpainted wood door opened just a crack. "*Jah?*" a woman asked.

"Hannah B—Lapp?" Emma asked.

"*Jah*, I am Hannah Lapp." Her accent was the same as the others' in town, though more pronounced—as if she didn't speak English much these days.

"And your maiden name was Beiler?"

"*Jah.*" She opened the door a bit more, but Emma was unable to make out her features in the dim light of the house.

"Are you the same Hannah Beiler who attended Rose Peterson's class on textiles at Hawthorne College in Massachusetts?"

"Maybe," Hannah hedged, but she let the door open a little more. "What do you want?"

Emma could just make out her face. Her blond hair was pulled back in the same manner as Casey's, though Hannah's seemed to not want to stay in place. Tendrils and wild strands stood out all around her head. Her eyes were blue and tired—or maybe they were sad. They matched the brackets at the sides of her mouth that weighed her lips down at the corners.

Her dress was dark and heavy looking, like the ones Emma had seen on the Amish women in town, though it seemed dowdier than the others. The apron she wore over her dress was black, but the cap on her head was a pristine white that seemed to clash with everything around it.

Although Hannah Lapp had aged considerably in the fifteen years since the college photo had been taken, Emma knew they were at the right place. Her heart beat a little faster in her chest.

"I'm Kelly, and this is Emma. Rose was our friend, and we're trying to find out more about how she died. Can we ask you a few questions?" Kelly stepped closer until she was almost side by side with Emma at the door.

Hannah shook her head. "I don't have anything more to say."

"Please," Emma said, doing her best not to seem desperate. "We've driven a long way to come talk to you."

"I'm sorry." She started to shut the door, but Emma stopped her, holding the door with one hand.

"Please," Emma said. "We just want to know the truth."

"I told the police everything I knew that night." But something flashed in her sad blue eyes. Regret? Recognition?

"There has to be something more, anything," Emma said.

"May we come in?" Kelly asked. "Just to talk about it a bit?"

Hannah shook her head. "I'm sorry for your loss, but I don't know more than I already said."

How were they going to get a DNA sample if they couldn't even get into the house?

"I would like to hear the story in your own words," Emma tried again.

"Those were my words on the police report."

Bathing a cat would be easier than this.

"From you directly," Kelly clarified.

A rustling sounded behind them. Emma turned to see a man standing in the entrance of the barn. Though he was several yards away, she could almost feel his steely gaze as he surveyed the scene on the porch. Despite the shadow the brim of his hat cast over his eyes, Emma could tell they were hard and unforgiving. She turned back to the front, suppressing a shudder at the appearance of such a granite-like man. Hannah's husband perhaps?

"Just a glass of—" Kelly wasn't able to finish the request. Hannah caught sight of something across the yard and shut the door in their faces.

Emma stared at windowless door that separated her from the last clue they had. "She knows more than she's letting on." Somehow she knew it, knew it in her bones. Just as she knew that Rose had been murdered.

Kelly shook her head. "Aside from breaking in, I don't see how we can get anything from her."

"Breaking in will be our last resort."

"Emma!"

"Just kidding. There has to be another way."

"Too bad there's not any laundry out here."

Too bad, Emma echoed in thought.

"Help you?"

They turned as the big Amish man came near. His beard was as scraggly and long as the mercantile owner's, and Emma wondered if that was a trait all the men here shared. No mustache, just whiskers—and bushy ones at that. He wore black pants held up by suspenders, black shoes covered in dust, and a blue shirt that had seen better days. By contrast, a beautiful horse trailed behind him on a lead.

"We came to talk to Hannah," Emma said, wishing they had taken a little more time to learn more about the Amish before coming here. She felt as if they had hit a brick wall of their own making. Were all the Amish this reserved? That would have been helpful to know going in. Horror of horrors—maybe she should have paid more attention to Dottie Faye's handout.

The man squinted at her in distrust. Weren't the Amish supposed to be hospitable? Amicable to the non-Amish, coexisting side by side? As it was, Hannah and this man were a matched set of misery.

"You friends of hers?" His accent was as thick as Hannah's. Emma could only assume that this man was Alvin Lapp, Hannah's husband.

"Something like that." Kelly stepped forward and held out a business card to the man. "I'm Kelly Grace. This is my business partner and friend, Emma Cotton. We were friends of the woman who taught Hannah at the college." Alvin Lapp refused to take the card from her, looking from it to each of their faces. Emma was waiting for him to spit on the ground, but it never happened.

"Are you Hannah's husband?" Kelly pushed the card into the back pocket of her jeans.

Alvin Lapp looked them over once again. His dark eyes appeared languid, but Emma had a feeling they didn't miss one detail.

His lip curled ever so slightly, almost imperceptibly. "*Jah*," he finally said.

"We would just like to talk to her for a bit."

Alvin shook his head. "If she wanted to talk, she would have let you in."

"We won't be long," Emma added. *Just long enough to get a DNA sample.*

A hairbrush—that was all they needed. One hair, and off to the lab it would go.

"It's a long ride back to town. Do you suppose we could use your restroom?" Emma asked.

Alvin nodded his head toward the side of the house next to the garden. "Outhouse is 'round thataway."

Outhouse?

"Oh, uh, thank you anyway," Kelly said, saving Emma the task of coming up with a suitable response.

"That's a beautiful horse," Emma said in a last-ditch effort to remain on the farm and possibly gain entrance into the house. If only she could talk to Hannah a bit more.

"*Ach*, it is at that." His eyes seemed to light up when he talked about the animal. Perhaps this was the way to get through to the man. He lovingly patted the beast on the neck, then smoothed a hand down its shiny coat, the action at direct odds with the stern set of his jaw.

"A Thoroughbred?" Emma asked.

He gave a quick nod. "You know about horses?"

Emma shrugged. "It's pretty obvious, such an exquisite creature."

"Right," he said, his eyes narrowing. For one moment he looked distrustful, and then it was gone. "Be mindful of the rut when you leave."

I guess that's our cue to go.

"Thank you for your time, Mr. Lapp," Kelly said, but he had already turned and disappeared back into the barn, the horse following dutifully behind him.

"So, I guess that's that," Kelly said, starting back to the Caddy.

"For now," Emma said.

They got into the car, and Kelly started the engine. Slowly

she turned the car around, avoiding the rut that Alvin had warned them about. She pulled the car back onto the road, but stopped and gave the house one last look.

Certainly it didn't look like any she had seen on the postcards and websites. There were no flowers planted around, just the garden filled with vegetables to feed the occupants. The barn where Alvin had been was painted white like the house and in need of a fresh coat just as badly. The fence surrounding the property, however, looked sturdy and strong, as if it was cared for regularly.

"Look," Kelly said as she started the car into motion once more.

In the pasture behind the barn, several horses munched on grass and rested in the afternoon sun. Their coats glistened in the bright yellow rays, their muscles playing beneath their skin like a well-rehearsed orchestra. Emma was sure she'd never seen a more beautiful sight.

"More Thoroughbreds?"

Kelly shrugged. "Seems sort of strange to me."

"Me too," Emma murmured. "How can the house be falling down around them and they have extremely valuable horses running around?"

It was a mystery, to be sure.

"You don't suppose he stole them, do you?" Kelly murmured.

The thought hadn't occurred to Emma. "I don't think so," she said truthfully.

"Why else would he be so distrustful of us?"

Emma laughed. "Look at us. Can you imagine what he thinks about us, showing up at his farm wearing jeans and T-shirts? He probably thinks we're the devil incarnate."

"I suppose," Kelly murmured as she negotiated the turn

that would take them back into town. "But there's something more here."

"Maybe," Emma said. It was true that Alvin and Hannah both seemed to have something to hide. But did that make Hannah guilty of murder?

"Maybe Dottie Faye found out something today."

"Maybe," Emma agreed, though she wasn't holding her breath.

"Hey," Kelly said, sensing her sadness. "You're looking at this all wrong. We found Hannah. That's big."

It was big, Emma agreed, but it wasn't enough. "Yeah," she said, trying to keep her voice upbeat. "Now all we have to do is figure out how to get close enough to her to get a DNA sample." One thing was certain: Hannah Beiler Lapp wasn't about to give it up willingly.

five

They arrived back at the Yoder B&B in time for tea. For once, Emma loaded up her plate as high as Kelly's and poured herself a cup of coffee. *Calories, shmalories*. She needed a treat, and she needed it now.

Dottie Faye was nowhere to be seen as they found a place to sit at the small bistro table in the common area.

"Well, that was a wash," Kelly said, slathering clotted cream on her scone.

Emma took a bite of her brownie. So maybe she hadn't gone all in like Kelly, but she was still on a splurge.

Jut like yesterday, today's choices were a strange mix of British and Amish food—apple crisp, scones, shortbread cookies, and buttermilk pie. All of it tasted like heaven.

"I followed him all afternoon, and he is definitely up to something." Dottie Faye appeared out of nowhere and slid into the seat opposite Emma. She gave a pointed nod to the man in the cowboy hat. "What did you find out from Hannah?"

"Nothing." Emma sighed. Less than nothing.

"But she's the right girl?"

Kelly nodded.

"I wouldn't call her a girl though," Emma added.

Dottie Faye waved a hand as if to dispel her words, then took a bite of apple crisp. "Yum-mee," she said with a theatrical roll of her eyes.

"She looked ... old," Kelly said thoughtfully.

Emma agreed.

"Like those girls who spend too much time in a tanning bed?" Dottie Faye asked.

Emma shook her head. "She seemed downtrodden and unhappy."

"Maybe she is," Dottie Faye replied.

"But that doesn't make her a murderer," Kelly said.

"It doesn't mean she isn't, either." Emma pushed her plate away, even though half of the brownie remained.

Dottie Faye shrugged. "Guilt can do funny things to a person."

"It was more than that. It's hard to explain, but she just acted weird."

Kelly nodded. "Like she was scared or something."

"Nervous," Emma added.

"I tell you, it's guilt." Dottie Faye finished her apple crisp and started in on the rest of Emma's brownie.

"I thought you were laying it all on him." Emma nodded her head toward Cowboy Hat Man.

"Well, I don't know if he had anything to do with Rose's murder, but he is definitely up to something."

Emma smiled despite herself. She was glad they had brought her aunt along. Dottie Faye might be loud and a handful, but she was always good for a laugh; and right then, that was just what Emma needed.

"But was it the mention of Rose's name or the appearance of her husband that had Hannah spooked?" Emma asked.

"He was something, huh?" Kelly said.

"Who?" Dottie Faye swung her gaze from one of them to the other.

"Alvin Lapp, Hannah's husband," Emma replied.

"What was strange about him?"

"He was …." Emma paused, trying to come up with the right words to describe the man.

"Intimidating," Kelly supplied.

Emma gave a nod of agreement. "And stern. He frowned the entire time we were there."

"Yeah, but that's not a crime," Kelly said.

"If it were, Tom Boyer would have to arrest himself." Dottie Faye laughed at her own joke.

"But he definitely made Hannah uncomfortable," Emma pointed out.

"He definitely made *me* uncomfortable," Kelly added.

"I thought we were going to get somewhere, and then he came out of the barn." Emma pulled her brownie back toward her and pinched off one corner. She popped it into her mouth and tried not to sigh as the flavor burst onto her tongue. Was this an Amish recipe or one from the English? She'd have to ask. "Has anyone seen Casey today?" Maybe she could shed some light on the relationship between Hannah and Alvin.

"She's off today," Dottie Faye replied. "I asked earlier."

"I was hoping she might know more about whatever it is between the Lapps. I mean, that was strange."

"I agree," Kelly said. "I thought for a minute that she was going to let us into the house."

"So no DNA sample?" Dottie Faye asked.

Emma shook her head. "Not even close."

"Hey, it wasn't a total loss," Kelly said. "We know we're on the right track. Now we just have to be patient."

But after fifteen years, patience was something Emma had only in short supply.

They finished their tea and decided to go back to the mercantile before it closed. With any luck, it wouldn't be quite so busy today, and they would have better opportunities to find out more about Hannah Lapp.

Again Emma marveled at how stepping into the store was like stepping back in time.

"Do you really think Alvin Lapp was serious about the outhouse?" Emma asked as they looked over the table of fabrics. The colors were dark and the swatches heavy, with not a pattern to be found.

Kelly shrugged. "I suppose he was. I mean, if the mercantile can't have power, what makes you think the houses have indoor plumbing?"

What sort of life was that for Hannah? She had come from an Amish home. Then she had gone out into the world with not just the basic conveniences, but things like cellphones and computers. What would drive a woman to come back into such primitive surroundings after tasting what the modern world had to offer? Guilt? Remorse? A secure place to hide? Familiarity? Genuine preference?

Kelly stared at the fabric Emma held in her hands. It was an ugly color with a dense weave, and it appeared to be the exact fabric that had made up Hannah's dress.

"Why would she do that?" Kelly asked, as if reading Emma's mind.

"I don't know." Emma gazed over at the shopkeeper to see if he was done helping his latest customer, only to find Dottie Faye already there.

"Why does the Amish bakery have power and you don't?" she asked without preamble.

The man blinked behind his glasses. "Because they are not really Amish, and I am."

Dottie Faye tilted her head to one side as if considering the facts. "I'm not sure I follow you. It says they're Amish."

"That's what they want you to believe."

"And they do this why?" she demanded.

"So you will buy their product. Tell me, did you come here to question the Amish or did you come to visit family or friends?"

"We came to find a—"

Emma cringed. Surely her aunt wouldn't blurt out their entire reason for coming to Fort Plain.

"We came to visit the Amish, naturally. One girl in particular," Dottie Faye said.

"Oh?" He raised one brow.

"Hannah Beiler. We asked you about her before. Well, she's Hannah Lapp now."

Emma watched the man carefully, gauging his reaction to Dottie Faye's revelation. If he was hiding anything, he didn't show it. And least not outwardly.

"Alvin's wife? *Jah*, I know Hannah Lapp."

"Does she come in here a lot?"

Something in his face seemed to shut down. "She comes in when she needs to, I s'pose."

"Dottie Faye," Emma called, "it's time to leave now."

"But I was just about to—"

Emma shook her head. "Let's go. Thank you, Mr. Yoder."

He nodded, but otherwise didn't respond, his mouth pulled down at the corners in disapproval. There'd be no getting any help from this man, and the last thing Emma wanted was to turn the whole community against them.

"Dottie Faye, we are supposed to be diplomatic," Emma said once they had stepped outside.

Her aunt shrugged. "I don't think handling a man like that with kid gloves will get us anywhere."

Emma shook her head, biting back further arguments.

"Where to now?" Kelly asked. "The diner?"

"Is that all you think about?" Emma asked.

Kelly shrugged. "It's hard to think about other things. This fresh country air has me starving."

Dottie Faye and Emma laughed, then the trio set out for the diner at the end of the block.

"Hey, let's go into the quilt shop first," Emma said as they approached Needles & Notions. They filed into the store, a tinkling bell signaling their arrival.

Unlike the mercantile, the store was well lit and cheery. Bright bolts of fabric in every available color and pattern stood in neat rows along the wall, three shelves high and nearly touching the ceiling.

Emma inhaled, deeply sucking in the familiar smells of dye and sizing. Suddenly she felt right at home, more so than she had since they left Mystic Harbor.

Dottie Faye pretended to look at buttons, but studied her manicure more than the product. Emma smiled. That was her aunt, loving to be in the middle of things.

Always working, Kelly immediately pulled out a business card and went to the counter, asking if the owner was available. How wonderful it would be to have their products in a store such as this. Their custom patterns were doing great, but Kelly took every opportunity to help them expand.

Emma was just about to join her when a familiar voice spoke behind her. "Emma Cotton?"

She turned to find Casey Yoder standing between the velvets and satins.

"Hi, Casey." She smiled at the young girl. After the sour faces of Hannah, Alvin, and the mercantile owner, Casey's sweet and open face was more than a welcome sight.

"Did you find Hannah Lapp?" Casey asked.

Emma nodded. "We did, but ...."

"She wasn't the right person?" Casey's smile twisted into a disappointed frown.

"No, she was the right Hannah, but she was reluctant to talk to us."

"Some Plain folk are like that," Casey explained, "especially around here."

"Why around here?" Emma asked.

Casey tilted her head to one side, the strings on her white Amish cap dancing around her slim shoulders. "We are what is known as Troyer Amish."

She really should have done more research before they'd left Massachusetts. Emma hadn't known that visiting the Amish could be as complicated as going to a foreign country. "What exactly does that mean?"

"That we are more conservative than most."

"More conservative than other Amish?" Emma asked.

"*Jah.*"

"So when Alvin Lapp told us there was an outhouse, he wasn't kidding?"

Casey shook her head and pressed her lips together. "So you met Hannah's husband, *jah*?"

"Is he always like that?"

"He is a very serious man."

Serious. Now there was a euphemism if Emma ever heard one.

"They say he is very mean to Hannah," Casey continued.

"Mean? How so?"

The young girl shrugged. "He is not a very kind man," Casey hedged, then she shook her head. "I do not think he likes her very much."

"But she's his wife."

"*Jah.*"

"If they don't get along, why don't they get a divorce?"

"Oh, no." Casey shook her head, the untied strings on her cap dancing once again. "The Amish never divorce."

"So, she's stuck with a man who doesn't even like her?" No wonder Hannah looked so sad. "He doesn't hurt her, does he?"

"It has not been said if he has."

Emma recalled the way he caressed the animal's neck. There was at least one redeeming quality in the man. "But the horses. He seems to treat them well."

"Oh, *jah*," she said. "He loves the animals, even though they don't belong to him."

Just then, Kelly strode up, smiling at the two of them. "I talked to the owner and got her card. When we get back home, we need to send her some samples. Hi, Casey."

"Hello, Kelly Grace."

"Casey was just telling me that the horses don't belong to Alvin Lapp."

"That explains a lot," Kelly said.

"If they aren't his, then who do they belong to?" Emma asked.

Casey bit her lip as if she realized she may have said too much. "I do not rightly know for certain, but there is a man who comes to town and stays for a while. I think they are his."

"That's very interesting," Kelly said.

Emma could almost see the wheels turning in her brain as she tried to figure out if there was any connection to Rose's case.

"Are you heading back to the B&B now?" Casey asked.

"Soon," Emma answered. "We thought we'd stop by the diner first."

"Uhum ..." Casey's face turned a bright shade of pink, almost the same color as the moiré she held in her hands.

"When you get back to the B&B, please don't mention that you saw me here. Please."

"Of course not," Kelly agreed automatically.

"Is something wrong?" Emma asked.

She shook her head. "It wouldn't be *gut* if my family knew I was here. Looking at the fabrics."

"Why ever not?" Ever tactless, Dottie Faye chose that moment to wander over and join in the conversation.

"They are forbidden."

"Fabrics?" all three of them echoed.

Casey solemnly nodded. "Such colors are against the *Ordnung*. Our rules," she explained.

"You have rules against fabric?" Dottie Faye asked.

Once again, Emma wondered what drove Hannah to return to such a strict society.

"Such fabrics are not humble. Flashy clothes and fabrics are prideful and vain."

Dottie Faye cleared her throat, but the gesture was lost on Casey.

"If they're against the rules, why are you here looking at them?" Kelly asked.

"I am on my *rumspringa*."

"What exactly does that mean?" she asked. Emma realized her ideas about *rumspringa* were about as vague as the rest of her understanding of Amish culture.

"When Amish boys and girls reach the age of sixteen, we are allowed to go out and experience the *Englisch* world."

Emma wouldn't have thought it possible, but Casey's color deepened. "There is a *bu*—a boy," she said. "An *Englisch* boy. He has asked me to something called 'the prom,' and I want to go so badly. I've been told I need a fancy dress."

Emma and Kelly nodded. "Most definitely," Kelly said.

Dottie Faye propped her hands on her hips. "Hold on a sec. I read that if you're Amish you have to marry another Amish, right? So, on your rum-thingie, you can date English boys?"

"*Nay*," she whispered. "Not really. That's why you can't tell."

"We won't say anything, sugar." Dottie Faye patted her arm reassuringly.

Casey let out a visible sigh of relief.

"One question," Emma said. "What happens if you fall in love with this boy, and you want to get married?"

Casey's eyes grew sad. "If I married him, then I would be shunned, and I would not be able to visit with my family."

Bingo. There was her answer. Love, the one reason Hannah would venture out into the modern world and family. And the only thing that would bring her back.

"Oh my stars and stripes," Dottie Faye said, startling Emma out of her train of thought. "Would you look at that?" She excused them from Casey and dragged Emma and Kelly away.

six

"Dottie Faye, was that really worth all that drama?" Emma asked, surveying with more than a little jealousy the selection of fabric before her.

Her aunt shrugged. "I thought it was. I mean, he's here."

"His *fabric* is here." Why did it seem like Emma was confronted with Antonio Roman's success every time she turned around? She couldn't even escape him in this Amish community.

"I think it's a sign," Dottie Faye said crossing her arms with emphatic purpose.

Kelly shook her head. "Of course they have Roman Originals here. It's a great shop."

Dottie Faye gave up her pose and trailed her fingers down the rich fabric. She studied it as if it held the secrets of the universe. "There's just something not right about this Antonio Roman."

"Roman?" Kelly snorted. "He's a—"

"Piece of work," Emma finished for her. And as much as she wanted to believe otherwise, Dottie Faye was right. There was something strange about the whole situation. If only she could figure out what.

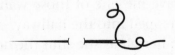

After going to bed early and sleeping soundly for once, Emma woke before the sun. She used the time to reflect on what they had discovered so far about Hannah Lapp. Zero. Really nothing. What she needed to figure out was how they could get close to her. Close enough to snatch a hair from her head.

Frustrated, she showered and was dressed by the time Dottie Faye and Kelly rolled out of bed.

"You're up early, sweet pea," Dottie Faye said with a small yawn. She had pushed her satin sleep mask to her forehead, the pastel pink matching the bows that adorned her silk leopard print pajamas.

"I slept well though." Maybe that was why she was up so early. She wasn't accustomed to getting so much uninterrupted rest.

"No dreams?" Kelly asked.

"None." That she could remember. At least she hadn't been haunted in the night by her lack of success concerning the case. Rose had been such a dear friend, and Emma felt as if she had let her down. Not to mention the guilt she carried around for talking Rose out of contacting the police before whatever was bothering her had turned to murder.

"I thought I might go down to breakfast early," she said, anxious to get a start on the day. She wasn't entirely sure it would help, but it beat sitting in the room and staring out the window wishing there were more for her to do.

"That's fine, dear," Dottie Faye said. "We'll get ready, then meet you in the dining area. How's that sound?"

"Good," she said, starting for the door.

"Be sure to save me one of those waffles," Dottie Faye called as Emma stepped into the hallway.

She smiled to herself as she shut the door on her aunt's request. Today was going to be a good day. She knew it. She willed it to be. She had searched and come up empty for too long now. Today was the day that would change everything.

Only a few of her fellow B&B guests were in the dining

room when she made her way downstairs. The man in the cowboy hat was nowhere to be seen. She poured herself a cup of coffee, taking a tentative sip to test its temperature before taking the healthy swig she desired.

She opted to wait on Dottie Faye and Kelly before eating and instead grabbed a morning paper from the table next to the buffet and found a chair.

Not much going on in the world, she thought, reading the headlines. A woman in a nearby town had miraculously found her class ring after it had been missing for nearly thirty years. Construction was continuing on the highway, and a man had been arrested under suspicion of doping racehorses.

At least there were no fallen soldiers, no six-car pileups, no school shootings. Not a bad day, news-wise. She took another drink of her coffee, wondering if anyone had worked the crossword puzzle. When the bell over the B&B door tinkled, Emma looked up to see who had arrived.

It was Hannah Beiler Lapp.

She was dressed the same today as she had been the day before—plain dress with an apron over the top. This frock was a dark purplish blue that would have been pretty had the fabric not been so heavy and dull. It matched her sad eyes. Hannah Lapp looked no happier today than she had the day before.

Over one arm she carried a large wicker basket, its contents covered with a striped dish towel.

"Hannah?" Emma stood. "Hannah Lapp?"

Hannah turned, and fear flashed quickly in her eyes. With her free hand, she reached up and patted her cap as if to check its placement, then she cleared her throat. "I told you all I know yesterday."

"I understand," Emma said gently, hoping to delay the woman long enough to figure out how to get DNA from her.

If only Kelly were down here with her! "I would still like to talk to you for a little bit. Can I buy you a cup of coffee?" Hannah shook her head and touched the handle of the basket where it lay over her arm. "I'm working."

"Oh?" Not exactly an earth-shattering idea on how to keep her there, but at least she hadn't run for the door.

"I sell eggs here."

Just then Mrs. Yoder came hustling in from the kitchen. "Hannah. There you are! Thank goodness. We're down to our last dozen. I was afraid that we wouldn't have enough for breakfast."

"I'm sorry, Sylvia. The hens were being stubborn yesterday." She shot Emma a look that somehow made it seem as if it were all her fault.

"Well, no matter now." Sylvia took the basket and handed it to one of the cooks who'd come out of the kitchen, most likely in hopes of receiving the fresh eggs before a guest riot ensued. Sylvia reached into the shelves behind the sign-in desk and brought out a small cashbox. She counted out the money to Hannah as Emma watched her chance of talking to her suspect slip away.

"You can come around the side and pick up your basket as soon as Debbie has it emptied."

"*Jah*," Hannah mumbled, her chin apparently stuck to her chest. "I will."

She turned to leave, but Emma couldn't let that happen. "Hannah." She followed her out the door and onto the porch. "Hannah, please. Talk to me for a bit. I only want to know more about my friend, and how she died. Surely you can understand that."

Hannah stopped, then turned to face her. "I know no more than what I've already told."

But she didn't look Emma in the eye as she said the words.

Emma recalled the spirited girl in the school photograph. What had happened to Hannah in the last fifteen years that had reduced her to a cowering mess?

Hannah glanced toward the street where a buggy waited. The reins were pulled through the opening of the carriage. There was no windshield to block her view, but the angle made it dark, casting shadows on the occupant. Emma didn't need to see to know that Alvin Lapp was in the driver's seat of the brown-topped buggy, waiting for his wife and watching their exchange.

"Please," Hannah said. "Leave me alone. I don't know anything more."

"Just a cup of coffee," Emma countered, not to be undone by the pleading in Hannah's voice. She had to do this. She had to do it for Rose.

Hannah stopped, but continued to face the street.

Emma could feel the other woman's resolve slipping. She was breaking her down.

"I have to go to the mercantile this afternoon to pick up some staples," Hannah murmured. Then, without a backward glance, she fled toward the buggy.

As much as she seemed afraid of her husband, Hannah Lapp seemed determined to stick by his side. *What a strange, abusive, symbiotic relationship they have,* Emma thought.

She watched the buggy pull away from the curb and out into the light morning traffic.

With a sigh, she made her way back into the B&B.

"Where have you been?" Kelly asked as she walked back into the dining area. Several more of the guests had come downstairs, including Cowboy Hat Man.

"I thought you were going to save me a waffle." Dottie Faye forked up a bite from the one on her plate with a wink.

"I just talked to Hannah Lapp."

"Are you kidding?" Kelly lowered her voice, but her excitement was evident.

Emma nodded. "Evidently she sells fresh eggs to the B&B."

"And they are good," Dottie Faye said, scooping up a bite. "So what did she say?"

Emma shook her head. "Nothing really. She stuck by 'I've told you everything I know' and 'I told the police all I could,' but I think she knows something more. She told me that she was going to the mercantile this afternoon."

"She agreed to meet us?"

"Not exactly. But I figure that has to be what she intended by telling me."

"Did you get a DNA sample?" Dottie Faye asked over the rim of her coffee cup.

"What was I supposed to do, pluck a hair right out of her head?"

Dottie Faye shrugged. "You could have asked."

"Yeah," Kelly said. "'You're a suspect in a murder investigation. Do you mind if I have a tissue or blood sample?'"

Dottie Faye shot her a frown. "That's not what I meant at all."

"I asked her to have a cup of coffee, but she refused."

"So, she's going to meet with us and perhaps tell us something," Kelly said, "but we still don't know how to get her DNA."

"I'm sure we can figure out a way," Dottie Faye said. "We just have to be creative."

But Emma was afraid they would have to be more than creative if they were going to break down the walls separating them and Hannah Lapp.

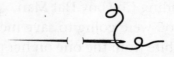

"Will you put those away?" Emma asked, trying hard to keep the exasperation out of her voice.

Dottie Faye lowered her opera glasses just briefly before lifting them to her eyes once more. "How else am I supposed to see when Hannah walks into the store?"

"We're across the street, not in the next county," Kelly said, suppressed laughter coloring her tone.

"Which is why I have my opera glasses and not my field binoculars."

Emma shook her head, but smiled.

They had taken up surveillance in the Laundromat across the street from the mercantile. She desperately wanted to talk to Hannah, perhaps get close enough to her to offer her some gum or buy her a lemonade in hopes of gaining their much-needed sample. But Hannah hadn't given her a time when she would be at the store, leaving them to wait outside until she arrived.

"Is that her?" Kelly tugged at Emma's shirtsleeve and pointed toward a lone Amish woman walking toward the store entrance. Her chin was down as if she needed to study her feet instead of where she was going.

"That's her."

"Let's go." Kelly slung her purse over her shoulder, but Dottie Faye waved them away with a flick of her hand. "Y'all go on ahead. I'll just stay here and watch."

Emma wasn't about to argue. She didn't have the time or the inclination to protest, though she thought perhaps Dottie Faye liked the idea of watching a suspect at least as much as actually tracking one down.

They stopped at the edge of the street, waiting as a horse-drawn buggy pulled past. Once again, Emma marveled at the beautiful horse used for such a task. She'd have to ask Casey if she knew anything about them. It just seemed as if there was some excellent horseflesh in town.

Once inside the mercantile, Emma blinked, her eyes adjusting to the dim light.

Mr. Yoder, the mercantile owner, frowned at them, but didn't stop helping his customer, an older lady dressed entirely in black. Her hands were gnarled from arthritis and her back was stooped. She needed quite a bit of assistance, which left Emma and Kelly free from the shopkeeper's interference.

"There she is." Kelly didn't raise her hand, but inclined her head toward the table of fabrics where Hannah stood.

Acting as if they had nothing but shopping on their minds, they made their way past the counter filled with old-fashioned candies. Emma stopped to examine a crate full of jelly jars while Kelly pulled an almanac from the bookshelf that lined the far wall. They pretended to browse for a few minutes more before easing their way toward the fabrics. "I was afraid you wouldn't come," Emma said, trying to break the ice.

Hannah turned away, flipping over a piece of fabric as if examining it for flaws. "I told you I would."

Like that made a difference. More than one of their suspects had said one thing and then done another. But somehow she knew Hannah meant what she said.

"You know something about the night Rose was—well, the night she died?" Emma had almost said "was murdered," but she had a feeling the word wouldn't sit well with Hannah.

"*Jah*," Hannah refolded the piece of fabric and flipped over several others until she came across a deep burgundy. At least Emma thought that was the color. With the natural lighting in the store only coming from the windows in front, it was hard to tell. "Rose's death seemed … unnatural. I mean, falling down the steps like that."

Good point, Emma thought. How many times a day did someone walk down those steps without it resulting in a cruel death?

Just then a woman came up. She was dressed much in the same way as Hannah, though she was as thin as a telephone pole. She had a hawklike nose and beady eyes that seemed to miss nothing.

"*Goedemiddag,* Hannah Lapp," the woman said, barely sparing Emma and Kelly a glance.

"*Goedemiddag,* Esther King." Hannah continued to ignore them, studying the fabrics as if her life depended on it.

Or did it? What if Esther King knew Hannah was talking to Emma and Kelly, these English tourists who had just come to town? Would she be in trouble with her church leaders? After the way all the Amish seemed to avoid contact with them, Emma was going with yes.

"It's a *gut* day to buy fabric, *jah*? Abner just told me he got a new shipment in yesterday."

Hannah nodded, but didn't respond to the woman. Somehow Emma got the feeling this one-sided conversation was less about niceties and more about power and control. Strange.

"Are you looking for something to make a new shirt for Alvin?"

Hannah looked down at the bright blue fabric she held in her hands as if seeing it for the first time. "Oh, *jah*. For Alvin." She faked a quick smile and set the fabric to one side. "Are you shopping for the bishop or the *kinner*?"

The woman, as if sensing they might be listening to the conversation, switched into the Amish native tongue, keeping her response from them. Still, Emma had heard enough. This woman was shopping for the bishop, which could only mean that she was his wife.

Kelly moved in close. "Isn't the bishop the leader of the church?" she asked so only Emma could hear.

"I think so."

Which meant they'd get no more information from Hannah until the disapproving woman left.

Emma and Kelly moved over to the bookcase to avoid raising Esther's suspicions any further. The volumes there were wholesome and classic. There was the Bible—well, she thought it looked like the Bible. It was written in a language that looked a little like German, but Emma wasn't entirely sure. The complete set of *The Little House on the Prairie* series was placed next to German titles she couldn't read. It was a small selection, but she acted as if each one was wholly interesting. She stayed close for her chance when Esther moved on.

Finally the woman selected her bolts of fabric and made her way to the counter.

Mr. Yoder turned his attention to Esther, but Emma had the feeling he was watching them more closely than he let on.

Emma moved back in. "So Rose's death wasn't an accident?"

Hannah shook her head. "But I didn't have anything to do with it." Her voice sounded small and more than a little worried.

"I was told you were seen glaring at Rose during your last class. And muttering?"

"It was a long time ago," Hannah said, as if that explained more than it really did. "I was angry with her for giving me a low grade on my project, but I didn't hurt her."

"Do you think someone pushed her down those steps?"

"I don't think it was an accident. *Nay*," she said.

"Did you see it happen?" Kelly asked.

Hannah shook her head again. "But there is one person who might have."

seven

There is one person who might have. The words ran like a hot iron through Emma's mind. *But who? Another of Rose's students?* But Hannah's words were cut short as the bishop's wife returned.

Hannah pressed her lips together so tightly that Emma wondered if she was trying to keep the words from escaping on their own.

Emma pulled another piece of fabric toward her, wondering why the Amish women accepted such thick and dreary fabrics as their fate. How did smothering yourself in your own clothes make you godlier?

She cast her glance sideways at Hannah, who was pretending that she didn't know Emma existed. Emma supposed that such interaction with non-Amish was frowned upon, or maybe it was the possible shame of her long-ago *rumspringa* that had Hannah hiding from the beady eyes of the bishop's wife.

"Any luck?" Emma jumped a little as Dottie Faye's voice sounded right behind her.

"No," she said. "I haven't been able to find the fabric I'm looking for." She raised her eyebrows for emphasis and hoped her aunt caught on. She didn't need her aunt scaring off the woman or drawing any more attention from the ever-watchful Abner Yoder.

"Oh." Dottie Faye gave an exaggerated nod. "I'll just be over here then," she said slowly, backing away toward the shelf of spices and dry goods.

Emma needed to finish her conversation with Hannah.

Not that she believed everything the woman said. She had been down this road with too many of Rose's students to take Hannah's word as gospel. Still, she wanted to know what it was that Hannah had been hiding for fifteen years.

Finally the bishop's wife went to the counter to pay for her purchases. Emma suspected that she was only trying to delay their conversation, as she didn't purchase any fabrics. With one last look at Hannah, the woman left the store.

Emma moved in closer to Hannah, lowering her voice as she spoke. "You were saying?" She didn't look up from the fabric she had spread across the table, though she cut her eyes toward Hannah. Was there a way to get a hair sample? Probably not with it twisted up under the cap like it was.

"I saw Rose at a pub the night before she died."

"Going to a pub is hardly a red flag," Emma said, then explained herself in case Hannah didn't understand. "It's not a problem that she went there."

In the sunlight, Emma could just see the glint of something on Hannah's shoulders. A hair! All she had to do was get a little bit closer, and she could snatch it off and send it to the lab. It wasn't optimum. The test was much more effective if the hair still had the root attached, but at this stage of the game she would take whatever she could get.

She inched toward Hannah who inched off in the other direction.

Be still, Emma willed.

"She was there with one of the other students," Hannah continued, once again studying the fabric. "And they looked like they didn't want to be seen."

"Still not an indication of foul play." Oh, how she wanted it to be. She moved a little closer, closer still until she could almost reach out and grab that little blond hair.

Maybe if she stretched. How much attention would that garner? Did she even care? Not if it got her the DNA sample she so desperately needed.

"Well, she and—"

"Hannah." She wasn't able to finish as a rather large, sour-faced woman called her name. The woman was dressed in the same manner as all the other Amish women they had seen in Fort Plain. Simple, hand-sewn dress of a dark, somber color, black bonnet, matching apron. And yet this woman seemed familiar somehow. "Hannah Lapp."

Hannah met Emma's gaze for a quick second, then abandoned the fabric to go to the woman's side.

And with her went Emma's chance of snatching the hair.

Hannah's face was stained with pink as she stood next to the large woman. "*Jah?*"

The words shot from the Amish woman's mouth like rapid-fire bullets. It took a moment for Emma to decipher that they weren't English. Whatever language she spoke was lyrical and a bit guttural, or maybe it was merely her tone. Emma didn't need to understand what was being said to know that the woman did not like Hannah talking to an *Englischer.*

Hannah dropped her head. The woman's tirade continued, attracting the stares of several other patrons.

Without a word in her own defense, Hannah allowed the woman to lead her from the mercantile. A hush fell over the customers as they watched her leave, then everyone went back to what they were doing, casting knowing glances at Emma as they continued to shop.

"Well," Kelly said, coming over to stand by Emma, "that was something. Wonder who she was?"

"Alvin's mother." Emma wasn't sure how she knew. She just did.

"Did Hannah say anything important before she left?"

Emma looked over to the mercantile owner who was staring at them, and not in a kindly way. "Time to go," she said. "Let's talk about this outside."

Hannah and her mother-in-law were nowhere to be seen.

Emma breathed a sigh of relief mixed with frustration. She had been so close to getting that sample, not to mention the name of the student who was with Rose and who might have witnessed her murder.

"Looks like a storm is coming in." Dottie Faye pointed toward the dark clouds gathering in the sky.

"In more ways than one," Emma said.

"Emma Jane, quit being cryptic, and tell us what she said." Kelly tugged on her arm for emphasis.

"Today the part of Dottie Faye will be played by Kelly Ann," Dottie Faye quipped.

Emma chuckled. "You two are priceless, you know that?"

Dottie Faye patted her big Georgia hair and flashed a beauty queen smile. "Yeah, sugar, I do."

"Let's head back to the B&B and see if we can make it in time for tea. I'll tell you everything when we get there."

But tea was over, and the trio found themselves once again seated in a booth at the diner.

"Tell me again," Kelly said, bracing her elbows on either side of her coffee mug and leaning forward as if that would help her understand Hannah's words better.

"I've told you three times already. I wish there was more."

"Me too." Kelly flopped back against the seat and pushed her hair out of her face.

"The worst part was that Hannah had this loose hair on her shoulder."

"Is that why you kept moving closer?" Kelly asked.

Emma nodded. "So close."

"So Hannah saw Rose at a bar—with a student—the night before she died?" Dottie Faye recounted.

"That's what she said." Emma folded a napkin like a fan for something to do with her hands. Her encounter with Hannah had left her anxious. Every heartbeat was just one step closer. So why did it seem like they were farther away from solving this mystery than they had been when they started?

"There you are!" Casey exclaimed, her voice breathless. "I've been looking all over for you."

"We've been right here," Dottie Faye said as if it were terribly obvious.

Casey flopped down on the bench next to Kelly. "I heard what happened at the mercantile."

"Word gets around fast." Emma unfolded the napkin and smoothed it with her hands.

"Oh, *jah*."

"So was that Alvin's mother who tore into her?" Dottie Faye asked.

Casey nodded. "She does not like Hannah very much."

"You think?" Kelly asked.

Casey nodded solemnly.

"Why?" Emma asked. "What did Hannah ever do to her?"

"I do not think Mary Lapp likes that her only son married Hannah."

"Why wouldn't she like that?" Emma asked.

Casey looked from side to side as if checking to see if anyone was close enough to hear her repeating gossip. "Hannah left the settlement."

"And that's not allowed?"

Casey shook her head. "We are a conservative people.

Most teenagers experience their run-around time at home, doing nothing more sinful than wearing jeans under their dresses."

"Oooh … scandalous!" Dottie Faye said.

Casey leaned in closer and lowered her voice. "It is a sin for sure and for certain to gossip, but I asked around like you said and heard she went to college."

Emma nodded. "She did."

"Schooling beyond what is allowed is prideful." Casey shook her head.

"So is being angry for getting a D on a class project," Dottie Faye said with a twist of her mouth.

"What?" Casey looked from Emma to Kelly.

"Never mind," Dottie Faye said. "Continue."

"Hannah didn't come back for years," Casey said.

"Is that bad?" Emma asked.

"Bad enough." Casey distractedly toyed with the salt shaker, obviously uncomfortable talking about such matters. "As I told you before, the part that upset everyone the most was that she had joined the church before she left."

A small frown knit Kelly's brow. "Why is that the bad part?"

"A person cannot go back on their commitment to God. Hannah joined the church and then decided she wanted to see more of the world."

"But she came back," Emma said.

"*Jah*, and she was shunned. She served her penance, but I do not think Mary Lapp ever forgave her as God did."

"Shunned?" Kelly asked. "What exactly does that mean?"

"It is how we bring a person who has strayed back into the fold." Casey went on to explain that shunned persons could not talk to the people around them until their shunning was over. They couldn't sit at the same table with others who were not shunned, and husbands and wives went as far as to sleep in separate beds.

"I'm sure that was effective," Dottie Faye drawled.

Kelly elbowed her in the ribs. "How long does a shunning last?"

"It depends on the sin committed. For Hannah, I've heard that it was a year, but I think the story has grown since it actually happened."

"A year?" Emma said. She realized she had attracted the attention of the others around her, so she lowered her voice. "A year?"

"It was likely no more than six months."

"Still," Emma said, "six months of having no one to talk to, not being able to be with the ones she loved." No wonder Hannah looked so downtrodden.

"The worst part of it all," Casey continued, "is that her parents both died when she was in her shunning."

"She never got to say goodbye," Dottie Faye murmured. Her aunt might be kooky and over the top, but Dottie Faye Sinclair had a big heart.

"Did she have any brothers or sisters?" Kelly asked.

"*Nay.* Most Amish families have seven or more children, but not Hannah's."

"What about Alvin?" Emma asked, wondering how Hannah's stern-faced husband fit into the story.

"She was not allowed to marry Alvin until the *bann* was lifted."

"Harsh," Dottie Faye said.

Again, Casey scanned the room to make sure no one was listening in. "I have this cousin, Ruth. She is about the same age as Hannah. She told me that once Hannah got back to the district, all the men her age were already married."

"So she married Alvin out of desperation?" Kelly asked.

"I guess so."

Emma recalled the hate she felt from Alvin's face as he drove away after delivering eggs to the B&B. He didn't seem to like Hannah much either. "But why did he marry her?"

Casey leaned in a little closer, the ties on her cap trailing along the tabletop. "If you ask the men, they will say that Alvin needed someone to cook and clean and take care of the woman's chores."

"I'm not even going to tell you how sexist that is," Dottie Faye said.

"But the women say that Alvin loved Hannah. Before she left, he was going to ask her to marry him. He was heartbroken when she jumped the fence and angry when she returned."

"He married her to be spiteful?"

Casey shrugged. "Some say he thought he would be able to forgive her over time, but instead he just got more and more angry."

"She has no recourse?" Dottie Faye asked. "No one should be married to a person who resents her."

"Not if she wants to remain with the Amish," Casey explained.

"When they say 'till death do you part,' they mean it." Dottie Faye signaled for the waitress to bring more iced tea. The conversation stalled as the woman refilled all the glasses, even bringing an extra for Casey.

Dottie Faye took a hesitant sip, then reached for the sugar packets. She mumbled something about Yankees under her breath as Emma hid her smile.

"But if he's mean to her," Kelly protested.

"I do not think he hurts her," Casey said. "Violence is against the Amish way."

"Still." Kelly frowned.

"Not everyone can have a husband like yours," Emma said, suppressing the tiny bit of jealousy that crept into her voice. She had spent all her extra time trying to figure out who had killed Rose. Even if she hadn't, she wouldn't have thought about love and marriage. In Emma's mind, it was her fault that Rose had died. It wasn't fair for Emma's life to go on while Rose's didn't.

"That's why I think you should see the good doctor," Dottie Faye sing-songed.

Casey's head whipped toward Emma in concern. "*Doktor?* Are you *grank?*"

"Am I what?" Emma asked.

"Sick?" Casey explained.

"No. Dottie Faye thinks I need a man in my life."

"Amen." Dottie Faye raised her glass in salute.

Emma shook her head.

"Marriage is a fine thing," Casey said, her voice somehow equally wise and naïve. Perhaps because she was parroting what she had been told her entire life.

"Hear, hear!" Kelly clinked glasses with Dottie Faye. Emma felt distinctly left out. It wasn't that she didn't want to be married. But it wasn't possible. Not now, anyway, and certainly not as long as Rose's killer was on the loose.

She would never admit it, but Dottie Faye was right; Dr. Eric Hart was perfect marriage material. But there was no way Emma would let her aunt know she felt that way. Emma would never hear the end of it.

"I have to go now." Casey stood and smoothed the front of her apron. "I told my aunt I would help her change the sheets in the Calico Room. We have new guests arriving at the B&B. *Danki* for the tea."

They said their goodbyes and watched as Casey made her way out of the diner.

"How old do you think she is?" Dottie Faye asked.

"At least sixteen," Kelly said. "Since she's 'running around,' as they say. Why?"

"She seems so young."

Emma nodded.

"Clean living," Dottie Faye added.

"What do you think will happen to her if her parents find out about her seeing this English boy?" Emma asked.

"They wouldn't approve, or she wouldn't be sneaking around."

"True," Emma said.

"I wonder if she's joined the church," Dottie Faye mused.

"Probably not, since she is running around," Kelly said.

Dottie Faye nodded and stirred her tea with her straw.

They fell silent as they each contemplated Casey's secret. She was such a sweet girl. Emma hated the thought of her getting into trouble over a guy, but people did all sorts of strange things for love.

"What do you think about Hannah's revelation?" Kelly asked, cutting through their thoughts and getting them all back on track after Casey's interruption.

Emma shrugged. "I don't know. Without a name, it's another dead end."

"She didn't know who it was Rose had met with?"

"Wait. That doesn't make sense. If she didn't know who it was, how could she know it was a student?" Dottie Faye asked.

"She never said she didn't know. She didn't have time to tell me. I don't even know whether it was a him or a her."

One step forward, half a step back.

eight

"And those are the new guests." Dottie Faye nodded toward two men standing near the buffet line.

"I suppose you think they're suspicious too?" Emma asked, looking up from the editorial page. She had taken to reading the local paper in the mornings. Mostly the news was refreshing instead of depressing.

"Well, they arrived in the middle of the night," Dottie Faye explained.

"That doesn't mean a thing," Emma said, hoping her aunt would drop it.

"How are we going to get a DNA sample from Hannah?" Kelly asked, thankfully changing the subject.

"You don't still think she's the murderer?" Dottie Faye's eyes widened in shock. Then she pulled her camera sunglasses over her eyes and trained them on the newcomers.

"No stone unturned," Emma countered.

"Exactly." Kelly popped the last bite of muffin into her mouth as Emma stirred the oatmeal around in her bowl. "We have to prove her innocence just as much as we need to prove the killer's guilt."

"There's just no getting close to her." Emma pushed the bowl of oatmeal away, too frustrated to eat more.

Kelly washed her muffin down with a sip of coffee. "Maybe we should head out to their farm again."

"And?"

"And wait until Alvin leaves. Maybe if he's not there, she'll talk to us."

"If nothing else, we can each snatch a hair from her head and run in different directions. She won't be able to catch all three of us."

"Last resort," Kelly said with a smile.

"We've been down here all morning," Dottie Faye said, turning off her camera but leaving the glasses firmly in place. "I don't think she's coming today."

"Maybe she's just late," Kelly said.

"Or maybe she delivers the eggs every other day."

Staking out her house was starting to seem like the only step they had left.

The bell above the door tinkled.

Emma turned toward the entrance hoping to see Hannah, but instead ... "Alvin Lapp." She nudged Kelly.

Alvin carried the same basket Hannah had the day before. He walked with a fiery purpose, the frown on his face pulling his eyebrows into one long dark line.

"Do you suppose he's forbidden her to come to town?" Kelly whispered.

"I don't know," Emma answered truthfully. If any or all of what Casey had told them was actually true, then it was very possible that Hannah had been instructed to stay out of town.

"Is he always like that?" Dottie Faye had started filming again. "So ... frowny?"

"I'm going with yes on this one," Kelly said.

They had no reason to believe anything else.

Sylvia Yoder bustled out of the back, faltering a bit when she saw Alvin standing there instead of Hannah. "Mr. Lapp." She cleared her throat and pulled the little cashbox out as she had with Hannah. But unlike the transaction with the man's wife, Sylvia didn't chastise Alvin for being late. She counted out his money, took the basket, and muttered a quick "thank you."

Alvin Lapp fisted the money in one hand and started for the door. Before he could reach the knob, it swung open. Another Amish man came in, a box of sweet-smelling pies cradled in his arms.

Seeing the newcomer and Alvin Lapp side by side, Emma couldn't help comparing the two. They were about the same build, though the baker was several inches shorter. Both had untrimmed beards without moustaches and black pants held up by suspenders.

Anger flashed in the baker's eyes. He seemed about to say something, then obviously thought better of it. Alvin seemed just as put out at being faced with the man and started past him, bumping shoulders as he tried to leave.

What was said next was anybody's guess. Well, anybody's who didn't speak Pennsylvania Dutch. It wasn't good, if their tones were any indication.

"I thought they were a peaceful people," Dottie Faye said.

Alvin Lapp was anything but peaceful in that moment.

Sylvia bravely stepped in between the two men, speaking the same language as she forced some space between them. She all but pushed Alvin Lapp out the door, then led the baker back to the check-in desk. She took the pies from him, set them on the stool behind her, and counted out his money, as cool as a cucumber. He said something to her in their language. Emma couldn't be sure what it was, but the tone was apologetic.

Sylvia nodded her head and walked him to the door.

"I'd give anything to know what they were saying," Dottie Faye mused.

"You and me both," Emma said.

Once behind the counter again, Sylvia moved the pies and collapsed onto the stool, laying her head on the desk with a heavy sigh. She stayed that way for a minute or so as the trio watched. Then she pulled herself together and hustled back into the kitchen.

"I wonder what Casey would say about that," Kelly muttered.

"I'd bet my favorite tube of lipstick she'll know something about it." Dottie Faye turned her attention back to the new guests, monitoring them in the suspicious act of drinking coffee.

It wasn't even nine o'clock. "It'll be hours before her shift starts," Emma pointed out.

Dottie Faye waved a hand. "Have another cup of coffee."

"Didn't Casey say the Amish are against violence?" Kelly asked, a puzzled frown marring her brow.

Emma nodded. "That's what she said."

"But it looked like Alvin ran into that baker on purpose, right?"

"Definitely," Dottie Faye answered, still eyeing the men at the table. They seemed to have noticed her attention and had turned a bit to block her view.

"Dottie Faye, please don't harass the other guests."

"I'm not harassing them." She turned to answer Emma, finally releasing the men from her steely stare.

"They might have something different to say." Emma nodded as the men stood, every so often casting glances at Dottie Faye as they gathered their things. "I would hate to get kicked out of here because someone complained."

"Oh, pooh." Dottie Faye pursed her lips in an exaggerated pout.

Kelly chuckled. "So what are we going to do today? We're not getting far with the townspeople."

Emma shrugged. "We could go look around the quilt shop some more."

"Or take one of those horse-and-wagon tours Sylvia told us about."

"That's not a bad idea," Kelly said. "It might give us some information on the community." Though that wasn't exactly what they needed. They needed a hair sample from a certain suspect.

"Did you see that collection box at the mercantile yesterday?" Dottie Faye asked.

"What collection box?" Emma hadn't gone near the counter. One, because the owner was glaring at her, and two, because she was more interested in talking to Hannah.

"It was up near the register. There was a little Amish boy, Joshua Beachey, who fell out of a tree and broke his neck. They were collecting money for the family."

"How sad," Kelly murmured.

"He looked to be about eight," Dottie Faye added. "The sign said he'd spend the rest of his life in a wheelchair."

Emma shook her head at the tragedy of it all. "So, how much money did you stuff in the box?"

Dottie Faye shrugged and turned away, feigning interest in the comings and goings of the older couple staying at the inn. Emma might have believed it if she were watching the man in the cowboy hat. But her actions only confirmed what Emma already knew. Her aunt was a big old softie.

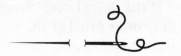

Four o'clock found the trio back in the B&B, hoping for a chance to talk to Casey. They had been all over the community, and though the day had been fun, it hadn't been productive toward their cause. It seemed everyone knew why they were there, or at the very least that they were asking questions and stirring up trouble. All the Amish and English people they had talked to had been more than nice and incredibly evasive. Their only hope now was Casey.

"There she is." Dottie Faye nudged Emma with her elbow.

Casey had just come out of the kitchen with a tray of cookies and was making her way through the room, passing them out to the guests.

"Would you like an Amish butterhorn cookie?"

"Do you have any peanut butter ones?" Dottie Faye asked. "Those are my favorites."

Casey shook her head. "We have a guest with an allergy. So no peanut anything for a while."

"I'll take one," Kelly said, waiting for Casey to hand her one of the crescent-shaped cookies from the tray.

They smelled delicious, like brown sugar and cinnamon.

"I was hoping we could talk to you some more today." Emma lowered her voice so that only the four of them could hear.

"About what happened at the inn this morning?" the young girl asked.

Emma blinked. "You know what happened?"

Casey nodded. "It was not the first time, I am sad to say. Those two have been at odds for a while now."

"Can we meet at the diner later?" Emma asked.

"I have to get my dress fitted at six. Maybe after that?"

"Your prom dress?" Kelly asked.

At the mention of the dance, Casey's eyes lit up. *"Jah."*

"About seven then?" Emma asked.

Casey nodded, handed another cookie to Kelly, and continued around the room.

Emma sighed. She recognized that look in Casey's eyes. There was nothing like young love. But this romance was forbidden, and she couldn't help but wonder if the young girl would end up as sad and bitter as Hannah Lapp.

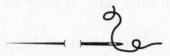

"You're saying there is no insurance for the Amish?" Dottie Faye looked stricken.

Casey took a sip of her Coke before answering. "We take care of our own. That is why there is a collection box. Plus the bishop will give the family some money. Friends and family will be by to help. Like when we have work frolics."

Dottie Faye shook her head as if she couldn't believe what she was hearing. Emma suspected there would be another large sum placed in the box in the not-so-distant future.

They had met over dinner, but the minute Casey walked in the door, their food was forgotten.

"What's a work frolic?" Emma asked.

"It is when the members of a district get together to help one particular family."

"Help them do what?" Kelly pushed her plate aside, then changed her mind and took one more bite of the meat loaf she'd ordered.

"Whatever needs to be done. Can food, build a barn, plant a garden, make a quilt, things like that. Sometimes they come to help with a new baby or clean for a church service."

Emma let that tradition sink in. How fascinating that the

Amish helped one another so willingly. What she wouldn't give to attend a work frolic where they made a quilt.

She caught Kelly's gaze and knew her friend was thinking the same thing.

"See, the boy's family will be OK," Casey said. "There will be a lot of help on their farm."

"Do all Amish have large families?" Kelly asked.

"*Jah*. Most families have at least six children. Sometimes more."

"But Hannah Beiler ... Hannah Lapp doesn't have any children at all. At least, there weren't any at the house when we were there," Emma pointed out.

"That is another sad story. It seems that the Lord did not see fit to bless Hannah and Alvin Lapp with any *kinner*."

Was that another reason for the downward turn at the corners of Hannah's mouth, or was her poor marriage the cause?

"Now, about this morning," Emma started.

Casey glanced around the room once again to check their privacy. "It is no secret that Alvin Lapp and Hannah are not a happy couple."

"But they can't get divorced because the Amish don't divorce," Kelly added.

"It is not our way." Casey frowned.

The waitress appeared to take away their half-eaten dinners and refresh everyone's drinks. "Did anyone save room for dessert?" she asked, looking at the food they hadn't eaten.

"Of course," Kelly said, shooting a pointed look at Emma.

Emma nodded. "Chocolate pie and coffee all round." She'd worry about those calories tomorrow as well.

The waitress gave a tiny nod and then went to get their dessert.

"So they're unhappy. What does that have to do with the baker?" Emma asked.

"Sometimes the members of the community will take into their own hands issues that the bishop might have overlooked," Casey explained. "Ben Lambright—he is the baker—he does not like the way the bishop has handled the problems between Hannah and Alvin, so he decided to put a personal *bann* on Alvin. He used to get all his eggs from Alvin, but now Ben refuses to buy from him."

"Which affects Alvin's income a great deal, I suppose." The peeling paint and worn-down look of the Lapp farm came to mind.

"*Jah.*"

"Are you saying that the bishop should talk to Alvin about how he treats Hannah?" Kelly asked.

How terrible that the troubles between Hannah and her husband were common knowledge throughout the community.

"*Jah.* For sure. Just because we are married for life does not mean we have to be miserable. There are ways for a couple to learn to get along."

"What happens if they don't? They just have to stay living together?" Dottie Faye shuddered.

"Well, if no other solution can be found, an Amish man or woman could move out of the house. Even then, they would not be able to get married again."

"Ever?" Dottie Faye's voice rang with shock.

"It is our way." Casey shrugged.

"So why doesn't Hannah leave?" Emma asked, recalling the sad look in the woman's eyes.

"I suppose because she has no place to go."

"So you're saying ...," Kelly prompted.

But it was Dottie Faye who answered. "Hannah's stuck with Alvin until one of them dies."

nine

"So what are we doing today?" Dottie Faye asked as she slid into the chair opposite Emma. Kelly was still at the breakfast bar, trying to decide between an apple fritter and a cherry scone.

Emma took a bite of her oatmeal and pretended it tasted better than it really did. "I'm not sure."

Kelly finally made her choice and joined them at the table. "Not sure about what?"

"I say we drive out to Hannah's and don't leave until we have that DNA sample." Dottie Faye took a quick sip of her coffee, then turned to watch the inn's most recently arrived guests as the two men made their way through the breakfast layout.

"What do you think?" Kelly asked Emma.

She shrugged. "I don't know what to do." She had been waiting in the common area of the B&B all morning, hoping and praying that Hannah would show. "Who knew it would be so hard to get close to one woman?"

"I know, right?" Dottie Faye took a quick bite from her toast, never taking her eyes off the men in their suits. "Don't you think that's a strange way to visit the Amish, in a business suit?"

Emma took a bite and resisted the urge to dump another packet of brown sugar into her bowl. "Maybe they're not here on vacation. Could be they really are here on business."

"But what *kind* of business?" Dottie Faye said, her eyebrows nearly disappearing in her hairline.

"Dottie Faye, can we stay on task here?"

Dottie Faye frowned at Emma but turned in her seat to face in the right direction. "Yes?"

"I guess we could go out there and see if Hannah will talk to us. I mean, what do we have to lose?" Emma asked.

"Or we could go out there and see if we can help her. Maybe that's the way to get to her?"

"Like the work frolic Casey was talking about?"

"Sure." Kelly shrugged. "Why not?"

Why not, indeed.

After breakfast the trio jumped into the car and headed for the country. It was another beautiful day. The sun shone on the green fields dotted with milk cows, sheep, and horses.

Kelly drove while Emma enjoyed the ride and Dottie Faye gawked at all the things she had missed by staying in town during their last trip to Hannah's.

"She lives out a ways, huh?" Dottie Faye asked as they turned off the main road onto the narrow country lane where Hannah and Alvin's farm was located.

"Have to have land to farm," Kelly pointed out. It was true. The houses had grown farther and farther apart the longer they had been in the car.

"Look, they have power." Dottie Faye pointed to a house with electrical wires running to it.

"Along with a car and a motor boat," Kelly added.

"I suppose not every farm out here is Amish," Emma mused. They had already passed three buggies and an old car.

"Sure is a lot of traffic today," Kelly said, nodding toward an approaching car, a silver sedan that looked out of place with its sleek lines and pristine finish.

The driver was going too fast and had decided to take his half of the road out of the middle, setting Emma on high alert.

"Is that a Mercedes?" Kelly asked.

Emma nodded, then swallowed hard. The car was still barreling toward them, still taking up both lanes.

They'd had too many brushes with death to not pay the car any mind. Surely their stalker hadn't followed them all the way out here. Did he want them off the case so bad as to track them all the way to New York State?

Kelly slowed the car and hugged the edge of the road as best she could. If she didn't do something fast, they were going to crash. She eased the wheels to the right. Emma thanked the heavens there was enough shoulder to support the Cadillac.

The Mercedes went flying by, missing them by what seemed to be inches. A miss was as good as a mile, but it was still too close for comfort.

"Are you OK?" Emma asked.

Kelly nodded as if she had just then realized she had stopped the car.

Emma was shaking from head to toe. *You're overreacting. Pull yourself together.* She hadn't been able to get a good look at the person behind the wheel of the Mercedes, but she breathed a sigh of relief that they had passed.

"Do you want me to drive?" Emma asked.

Kelly nodded as the buggy they had just passed caught up with them. The man pulled to a stop in front of them and got out.

Emma rolled down the window and waited as he approached. "You *allrecht*?" He leaned down and peered into the car, his long beard bobbing with every syllable.

Like Alvin Lapp and the baker, he wore black pants with suspenders to hold them up. His shirt was a soft shade of green that made his warm brown eyes seem friendly and caring.

Kelly nodded and tried a smile. It trembled on her lips,

but she managed to pull it off. Well, at least enough so the man gave a nod in return.

"Did you see a silver car?" Emma asked. Maybe the Mercedes had passed the buggy while traveling as erratically as when it had passed them.

"*Jah*. Driving like maniacs. Never seen them around these parts. They friends of yours?"

"They scared the bejeebers out of us," Dottie Faye said. "We just stopped to get our breath back."

"You are all right, then?"

"Right as rain," Dottie Faye said.

If Emma didn't know better, she would have thought her aunt was flirting with the man, but that was impossible. Not that he wasn't handsome enough for a woman to flirt with, but flirting with an Amish man was a stretch, even for Dottie Faye.

"Do most out-of-towners drive that fast around here?" Emma asked. "Don't they realize they have to share the road with your buggies?"

"Not all, but some," he said. "You may have heard of Amish buggies being hit by an *Englischer's* car. Sometimes it kills our horse. Sometimes it's worse."

"How horrible," Kelly said.

"*Jah*. It is something we must deal with."

"We have an Amish friend," Emma said. "We try to keep that in mind as we drive through your communities."

"For that I am grateful." The kind man touched the brim of his hat. "*Ach*, then. I will leave you to your day."

Emma rolled up the window, grateful that the silver Mercedes had avoided them all.

"Are you ready?" Kelly asked.

"I thought you wanted Emma to drive," Dottie Faye said.

Kelly shook her head. "I'm OK now." She eased the car back onto the narrow road.

In her rearview mirror, Emma saw the buggy pull out behind them. There were two gentlemen inside, the driver and another man who looked as sour-faced as the bishop's wife.

But the tone of the trip had changed, and silence reigned the rest of the way to the Lapp farm.

"This is it?" Dottie Faye asked as they pulled into the hard-packed drive.

"Yep." Emma put the car in park and cut the engine. The farm looked just as bad today as it had before, as run-down and neglected as ever. With one big difference.

"Oh, my lands." Dottie Faye got out of the car and pointed to the porch.

A man lay in the doorway, half in and half out of the house. Judging by his size, it was Alvin Lapp.

"Why does this keep happening to us?" Kelly asked, releasing her seat belt and jumping from the car.

"I wish I knew." Emma was out of the car and running to the porch. "Please don't be dead, please don't be dead, please don't be dead."

Yes, it was Alvin Lapp, his eyes open and staring at nothing.

Dottie Faye knelt and pressed two fingers to the man's neck. "He's dead," Dottie Faye said, looking at each of them in turn.

Kelly gasped and clamped her hand over her mouth.

Emma sighed and shook her head. This was not good.

She glanced inside the house, unable to look at the body any longer. Where was Hannah?

"He's not shot or anything," Dottie Faye said, slipping into full-blown CSI mode.

"Don't touch anything," Kelly warned.

Emma shuddered, then took a step toward the house.

Best to pretend there wasn't a dead body on the porch and instead hope the person responsible wasn't lurking around somewhere, waiting on another opportunity to strike. *You've been watching too much TV.*

"Hannah?" she called hesitantly.

"Do you think he was murdered?" Kelly asked, her voice trembling.

"Of course he was murdered!" Dottie Faye exclaimed.

"Hannah?" Emma eased into the house, surprised by how much natural light filled the space. She stepped into the living room as Dottie Faye and Kelly continued to talk behind her.

"Call 911," Emma said as she surveyed the room.

She heard Kelly rush off the porch as she went to retrieve her phone from the car.

The room was plain. It was as simple as that. No pictures on the walls, no rugs on the floors. No curtains on the windows, which explained the lighting.

"There's pie out here." Dottie Faye said. She pointed to what was left of a piece next to Alvin's body.

"Pie?" Emma ventured farther into the house. On the other side of a wooden bench that she supposed passed for a couch was a sturdy-looking wooden table.

"Yeah, it looks like he was eating a piece of pie when he died," Dottie Faye said.

"Do you suppose he fell? Maybe hit his head?" Emma asked.

Kelly's voice floated in from the outside. She had reached someone on the emergency line and was struggling to keep her composure as she detailed what she saw.

"I think he was poisoned," Dottie Faye concluded.

Emma resisted the urge to sigh. That was just her aunt's way, melodramatic to the end. But these circumstances allowed for Dottie Faye's theatrics.

"They're sending someone out," Kelly said ahead of a deep, shuddering breath.

"That's good." Emma walked back onto the porch to join them.

"Is Hannah in there?" Kelly asked.

Emma shook her head. "I didn't check all the rooms."

"Do you think she did this?" Dottie Faye asked.

"Nothing was 'done,'" Emma said emphatically, though she was beginning to have her doubts.

"Do you think Hannah is around somewhere?" Kelly's gaze scanned the yard. To Emma, nothing seemed out of place, nothing out of the ordinary.

"I'll check the other rooms." If Hannah was there, they needed to find her.

"I don't suppose we can leave before the authorities show up," Kelly mused.

The sight of Alvin Lapp dead on his porch was quickly becoming more than they could bear. Emma couldn't blame her friend for wanting to leave, but she shook her head.

"I'll search the barn," Kelly said.

"I'll stay right here." Dottie Faye plopped down onto the thick wooden rocking chair, but Emma noticed that she stared at the pecking chickens instead of the wide eyes of Alvin Lapp.

"We need your help," Kelly said, using the magic words that were certain to get Dottie Faye on her feet.

"I'm needed here."

"Why?" Kelly asked.

"Well, somebody's got to guard the body."

"Dottie Faye, there's no evidence of foul play," Emma said. She said the words, but something about the situation just wasn't right.

Her aunt harrumphed. "A man's dead. That's foul enough for me."

Emma didn't want to argue. They were all in a bit of shock. Only two days ago, the man had been standing right there in the yard, scowling at them.

Kelly gave a little jerk, a cross between a nod and a shrug, and started for the barn. Emma turned and made her way back into the house.

The layout was simple, with two bedrooms side by side down a short hall. There was no bathroom, which she supposed meant the house had been specifically built for a conservative Amish family.

She checked under each bed, but not even dust bunnies crouched there. Hannah Lapp might be poor, but she was clean.

"Emma," Dottie Faye called from the porch. "Do you think you could find a towel or something?"

"A towel?" She stood and brushed nonexistent dust from the knees of her jeans.

"I'm a little uncomfortable with him staring at me."

"Right." She looked around the room. There were no closets, just pegs on the wall where clothes hung as if waiting for their owners to return. A cedar chest sat at the end of the bed. Emma opened it to find extra quilts and a sheet. She took the latter out front and gently laid it across Alvin Lapp's body.

"Thank you," Dottie Faye said.

It was the least she could do for both of them.

Back in the bedrooms, Emma noted only one room's pegs held clothes, and all of those appeared to belong to Alvin. Emma could only suppose that room was the one Hannah shared with her husband, but it certainly didn't look like it.

What was keeping the sheriff? She wanted nothing more than to get back into town and away from the tragedy that had befallen Alvin Lapp. Emma made her way back down the hall.

Her aunt was rubbing off on her. It was tragic that he had died; the man couldn't be over forty years old, if even that. *But there are no obvious indications of foul play,* she told herself. Emma walked back into the front room of the house. *He fell, or maybe he had a heart condition.*

In the kitchen area, half of a cherry pie sat in the center of the sturdy wooden table. Two plates, one holding a piece of pie and one empty, sat at opposite ends of the rectangular table. The third piece was with Alvin on the front porch. But where was Hannah?

Emma stepped into the cooking area, certain she had been transported into the kitchen from *Little House on the Prairie.* There was no coffeepot, no blender, nothing modern at all. An antique-looking icebox crouched in one corner and a wood-burning stove in the other. Surely Hannah didn't use them. But Emma saw no other way to keep food fresh or cook it.

On the far side of the room, past the calendar with a picture of a horse on it, was a door.

Emma approached it cautiously. "Hannah?" she called softly. No answer.

She rapped lightly on the wood, and a small scratchy sound was the only response.

Emma gently turned the knob and eased into the room. A plain wooden bed filled most of the space. Like the other bedrooms, a beautiful quilt served as a duvet, the colors gleaming even in the room's dim light. The quilt was the famous double wedding band pattern, and for a moment, Emma wondered if it was something Hannah herself had made for her wedding to Alvin. The large scalloped edges nearly touched the wide planks of the floor.

There was only one window in the room, and it wasn't large enough to fill the small space with light. A pegboard where dresses and aprons hung told the real tale of the Lapp household. Hannah's clothes were in here, while Alvin's were in the other bedroom. Not a good sign for a marriage.

There was the noise again, almost like a rasping. Emma took a cautious step forward. It came from under the bed.

Heart beating faster, she dropped to her knees, unsure of what she would find. Slowly she lifted the quilt to peer underneath.

Something flew out from under the bed, hissing and spitting as it dashed under a rocking chair, the room's only other piece of furniture. Emma screamed, scrambling to her feet as she tried to get back her wits.

She clamped a hand over her mouth and turned to see what had terrified her so.

A large calico cat sat under the chair, glaring at her with wide green eyes.

"Kitty," she breathed.

The cat hissed.

"Emma, are you OK?" She heard Dottie Faye and Kelly a moment before they burst into the room.

"Just surprised was all." All of her aunt's theories had her as jumpy as … well, as a cat.

The feline hissed again with an angry flick of her tail.

From outside, Emma heard the sound of crunching tires, a humming engine, and then the slam of a car door.

"Did you find Hannah?" she asked Kelly.

Her friend shook her head as Dottie Faye stepped out of the room. "Are you sure you're OK?" Kelly asked.

"I'm fine," Emma answered.

Dottie Faye stepped back into the room, her mouth pulled into a grim line. "Sheriff's here."

ten

Heart still pounding in her throat, Emma stepped into the front room of the house with Dottie Faye and Kelly close behind her.

The sheriff was on the porch, kneeling by the body. Dottie Faye, it seemed, was unable to stand Alvin's body even covered with a sheet and had pulled his hat over his face as well.

The lawman caught sight of them and touched his gun butt. Seeing that they weren't a threat, he went back to his assessment. His bulky form kept them from exiting the house. They stood, gathered at the threshold, waiting for him to finish examining Alvin. "Sheriff Roy Johnson." He stood, extending his hand for them to shake in turn. "You found the body?"

"Yes." Kelly swallowed hard and looked away. Emma understood. They had seen enough death.

"The body was just like this?" the sheriff asked.

"We covered him," Emma explained.

"And his hat," Dottie Faye added. "It was over that way." She motioned with one fluttering hand.

He nodded as if he understood.

Another car approached. Emma looked out the front window to see a deputy pull his service vehicle into the drive.

"Can we go?" Dottie Faye asked, nodding toward the door.

The sheriff shook his head. "Not until I get your statement."

"Outside," she clarified. "I don't like standing in here and ..." She shuddered.

The sheriff allowed them to pass.

It was creepy, stepping over a dead man. Sure, Emma had stepped over him to get into the house, but she hadn't been thinking about it then. She had been too worried about Hannah.

"Go over there and stand by my car. I'll be along shortly to talk to you."

Quietly, the trio made their way to the sheriff's SUV. Emma leaned against the fender. The deputy approached the porch, and the two men got down to the business of investigating what had happened.

"I wonder where Hannah is," Kelly whispered so only the three of them could hear.

"I wonder how she's going to take this," Dottie Faye countered.

"You don't think she did it, do you?" Emma looked at each of them in turn. "I mean, the only way out of her miserable marriage is ..." She looked back to the porch and the hulking form of Alvin Lapp. "... death."

Please let it be natural causes.

The click of horse hooves sounded behind them along with the creak of a buggy and the rattle of horse harnesses. The same buggy that had stopped to help them pulled into the drive behind the deputy's car.

"*Ach,*" the brown-eyed man said in lieu of a greeting. He swung down from his buggy and came to stand beside them. "What has happened here?"

"Maybe you should talk to the sheriff about that." Emma indicated the two men on the porch; the sheriff was once again crouching by Alvin's body. She had no idea what she should tell the man. She was probably on the list of suspects. Well, at least until they ruled out foul play.

Please, please, please, not murder. She had seen enough of that to last a lifetime.

The man nodded and made his way to the porch followed by his passenger. Their clothes were mirror images of each other, but the men themselves couldn't have been more dissimilar. Whereas the driver was solid looking, strong, and capable, the other man appeared frail. Almost sickly. One had dark hair, the other blond. Only the driver spoke.

As they watched, the sheriff stood. He adjusted his hat and stared at the sun as if the answers were written in the sky.

"Something's not right," Emma mused.

Bits and snatches of the conversation floated toward them as the sheriff and the driver continued to talk. Words like "horses," "bishop," and "tragic" were spoken. But that was all Emma could make out clearly.

She continued to watch as the men glanced from the pasture to the dead body.

"I wish I knew where Hannah was," Kelly said.

"That makes two of us," Emma muttered, as once again the sound of a car engine and the crunch of tires were added to the rustling of the wind and the songs of the birds in the trees.

The coroner had arrived. He got out of his long white station wagon, a black bag in his hand. He was by far the oldest man there, his white hair and neatly trimmed goatee giving him a wizened air, though his denim overalls distracted from the look. He greeted them with a brief dip of his chin and joined the others surrounding the body. Everyone stepped back to allow him room to work. The move also put them a little closer to the women, but not by much.

As if drawn by a string, Emma pushed to her feet and crept closer to the men.

"Do you suppose now we'll be able to talk to Hannah?" Dottie Faye asked.

"Dottie Faye," Kelly chastised.

Emma inched closer to the men.

"I didn't mean it that way," Dottie Faye said, pouting. "You were the one who said you thought Alvin was the reason she wouldn't talk to us. Well, now he's dead."

"Shh," Emma hissed.

She needed to hear what the men were saying.

"Natural causes," the coroner said, taking his stethoscope from his ears and hooking the device around his neck. He pulled up the man's wrist and pressed his fingers to it as if checking for a pulse.

"Natural causes?" Dottie Faye blurted out.

"*Jah,*" the Amish driver said. "The coroner has confirmed, and the bishop and I agree."

"The bishop?" Emma asked.

"*Jah,*" the frail blond man stepped forward and tipped his hat. He didn't look like any minister Emma had ever seen, but he was Amish, and she only had her own experience to go off of. "I am Bishop King."

"Bishop King? You're Esther's husband?" The image of the sour-faced woman popped into Emma's mind. The couple were about as mismatched as he and the driver.

"*Jah.*" His eyes narrowed. "You know my *fraa?*"

"We saw her in the mercantile," Kelly explained.

He gave a small nod of understanding, but questions still lit his brown eyes.

"Natural causes," the sheriff said to his deputy. He pulled off his hat and ran the back of his arm over his forehead.

The deputy nodded, taking notes in a tiny notepad with a spiral at the top.

"Natural causes?" Dottie Faye cried again. "How do you figure that?"

The sheriff's eyes narrowed, and for a moment, Emma thought he would ignore her aunt's question. Then he looked from Emma to Dottie Faye and Kelly, who had come up behind her. "Simple, Miss …?"

"Sinclair," she said. "But you can call me Dottie Faye. This is my niece, Emma Jane Cotton, and her friend, Kelly Ann Grace."

"I don't believe I've ever seen you around these parts. Are you friends of Alvin's and Hannah's?"

"Sort of," Emma said, hoping he didn't hold her to it.

"Well, Ms. Sinclair." He adjusted his gun belt and looked down his nose at them. Emma supposed he might have been considered a handsome man if he hadn't had the disdainful sneer and cold blue eyes. "There is no evidence of foul play."

"So he what? Had a heart attack?" Dottie Faye asked. Her voice rose an octave, a sure sign she was gearing up for a fight.

This should be interesting.

"Most likely, yes," the sheriff said.

"At his age? What is he, like, thirty-five? thirty-six?" Kelly asked.

"I believe he's closer to forty," the bishop said.

"Still. Forty," Dottie Faye said. "Who has a fatal heart attack at forty?"

Emma felt all of her prayers slipping away. This was not going to be easy.

"It's not unheard of," the coroner explained.

Then it clicked, all the things wrong with the scene. "He's lying in the doorway of his own house. And he's been eating pie," Emma pointed out.

The sheriff raised one brow. "Eating pie doesn't cause death."

"But who eats pie walking around?" Emma asked.

"The Amish do. Quite a bit. They have chores to see to,

Miss Cotton. They make their pies with extra-thick bottom crusts so they can carry the slice in their hands and eat it while on their way to the next chore."

"But he's barefoot," Dottie Faye pointed out. "You mean to tell me he's going to walk around a barnyard with no shoes on his feet?"

"I do." He gave a stern nod. "The Amish don't always wear shoes in the summertime."

Behind him the bishop and his Amish driver nodded in agreement.

"What about the two plates on the table?" Kelly pointed out.

"Yeah," Dottie Faye said, backing her up. "If he was going to walk around with his pie, how come he got a plate too?"

"And who was eating there with him?" Emma asked.

"Or sitting with him? Whoever it was didn't eat anything," Kelly added. "The other piece of pie is untouched. And as we were coming out to the farm, we were nearly run off the road by a car speeding away from here."

"Now just hold on a minute." The sheriff held his hands up in front of him as if to stave them off.

But the coroner stood and stroked his chin whiskers. Unlike the Amish men, his beard included a moustache. "Well now, Roy, this might be a problem."

The sheriff turned to him. "You think?"

He nodded.

The deputy looked back to the body, then stepped over toward the debate brewing in the front yard. "Why are you all here?" he asked, pinning them all with an accusatory stare. "Did you have a beef with Alvin Lapp?"

"We don't even know the man, copper." Dottie Faye propped her hands on her hips.

Emma pinched her aunt.

"Ow." Dottie Faye rubbed the spot and glared at Emma.

"We came out here to see Hannah," Emma explained.

"So you're friends of hers?" the sheriff asked again.

"We have a mutual friend," Kelly hedged.

"If you're here to see Hannah Lapp, then where is she?"

"We don't know." Emma tried her best to make her voice sound confident without being defensive. "We couldn't exactly call her on the phone to let her know we were coming."

As if there weren't enough people already on the scene, Emma turned as she heard the now-familiar sounds of a buggy coming down the drive.

Without a glass windshield to hide her from view, Emma could see Hannah Lapp driving. She slowed the horse as soon as she caught sight of the sheriff's car.

"There she is," someone said.

They watched as she pulled to a stop. Slowly she slid the door open and stepped to the ground.

She looked around the faces all staring at her. *"Was iss letz?"*

In response, the men moved closer together to block her view of the dead body of her husband. Their efforts came a little too late.

Hannah looked from Alvin to the men, her forehead puckering as she continued toward the house.

Emma watched, unable to take her eyes from the woman as she approached. She had a feeling there was no love lost between Hannah and Alvin, but she had lived with the man for years. It would have to be a shock to see him lying dead on their front porch.

But Hannah's face was unreadable as she gazed at her husband. "Is he dead?" Her voice carried no trace of emotion. Her shoulders didn't tremble with shock or sobs.

She merely stared at him as if looking at someone she had never seen before.

"Yep." The sheriff looked to the coroner, then back to Hannah. "You been gone long?"

Hannah shook her head then changed her mind and nodded. "A while," she whispered. It was the first sign of upset that Emma had seen from her.

"Where'd you go?" The deputy flipped to a new page in his notebook and held his pen at the ready.

"Down to the cemetery."

The bishop crossed his arms and huffed. "Hannah Lapp, you know we don't visit the dead."

She opened her mouth to say something, then closed it and dropped her chin to her chest.

"Anyone see you there?" The deputy tapped the end of his pen on the notebook and waited for her answer.

She shook her head.

"Stay here." The sheriff stepped over Alvin's body. Emma resisted the urge to scream at him not to do that. It was unnerving the way they disregarded him.

She could hear the sheriff in the kitchen. From his footsteps on the hard wooden floor, she imagined that he walked around the table.

The deputy peered through the doorway, then turned his attention back to Hannah as if she were about to take flight.

The sheriff appeared back at the doorway. "You say you were at the cemetery?"

Hannah nodded.

"He was like this when you arrived here?" This question was directed at Emma.

"Yes," Emma said.

As he mulled over their answers, the calico cat that had

scared Emma half to death appeared around the side of the house. She sauntered over to Hannah, who reached down and scooped the cat into her arms, lovingly scratching the feline behind the ears.

"Tell me again. Why are you here?" the sheriff asked.

"We came to visit with Hannah," Emma said, the line of questioning beginning to grate on her nerves.

"I see." He took out a small notebook of his own and started writing in it. "We'll need witness statements from all of you. You have your IDs, correct?" He shot them a grin, like one would give a small child.

They nodded.

Despite the warm sunny day, something about the man's smile sent chill bumps chasing up her arms.

"Dale, you see to it that these ladies fill out the proper paperwork."

"Yes sir." The deputy started toward them, motioning them to follow him back to his car.

Emma wanted to protest. She was so close to Hannah, she might easily have reached out and plucked a hair from her unsuspecting head. But even her commitment to find Rose's killer wasn't strong enough to do that to a woman who'd just lost her husband.

Dottie Faye and Kelly started toward the car.

"Come on, Emma Jane," Dottie Faye said, her voice strangely soothing. But something in Emma didn't want to leave Hannah.

"Miss Cotton," Dale the deputy said, his tone urging her to comply. Emma started back toward the car, her steps in reverse, as she watched the sheriff raise his eyebrows at the coroner.

Something was up.

"Well, Bill?" the sheriff asked.

"I don't know, Roy. Could be poison."

The sheriff nodded. "The pie."

Hannah continued to pet the calico.

Hadn't Dakota Longbone in Arizona told them that Hannah made the best cherry pies? Had she made the one on the table?

"We'll have to do an autopsy," Bill the coroner said.

Both the Amish men started to protest.

The sheriff held up his hands to calm them. "Now, now, hear me out. If this is foul play, we need to be certain."

"It is not our way," the bishop said.

Behind her, Emma heard the deputy instructing Dottie Faye and Kelly on how to fill out the report.

"Neither is murder," the sheriff said cryptically.

"What?" the bishop asked.

The sheriff turned to Hannah and removed the cat from her arms, setting the beast on the ground at her feet. "Hannah Lapp," he said, "we're taking you in for questioning."

eleven

Everything seemed to happen at once. The Amish men protested loudly in Pennsylvania Dutch. The sheriff pulled out his handcuffs as he explained it was for her "own protection." *Yeah, right.*

"Wait." Emma broke away from the deputy and approached Hannah as the sheriff snapped the cuffs onto her wrists. At her feet, the cat mewed as if she knew something wasn't right. This was not what Emma had in mind when she insisted that Alvin had been murdered.

"Now, missy." The sheriff took Hannah by the elbow and led her to his SUV.

She looked as stunned as Emma felt.

Emma could only imagine what was going on in her head. She had to be scared to death. "Are you arresting her?"

"You get back over there with your friends, or you'll find yourself in this car right along with her. Mind your head," the sheriff said as he helped Hannah into the back of the patrol vehicle.

He shut the door of the SUV with a decisive *thunk*, leaving Emma feeling helpless and a little responsible.

Hannah didn't cry. She didn't break down. In fact, she showed no emotion whatsoever. Her husband had been murdered, yet she looked like she was about to take a stroll with friends.

Was it shock or relief that had her seeming so serene, so distant?

Unable to do more, Emma backed away to stand by Dottie Faye and Kelly.

"Dale," the sheriff called. He stood in the open door of his SUV. "As soon as Joe gets here, bring these ladies on into the station and get their statements. And have someone drive their car back to town."

"What about the bishop?"

The sheriff shook his head. "They came after we had already arrived on the scene. No need to detain them any longer." He tipped his hat to the two Amish men and ducked inside his truck.

"Great," Kelly muttered.

"Exactly," Emma said.

Dottie Faye turned toward them, her eyes lighting with something Emma wasn't sure she wanted to see. "Wait a minute. If Hannah killed her husband, isn't it likely that she killed Rose too?"

"Of course not," Kelly said, but Emma was beginning to have her doubts. Could Hannah have killed Alvin *and* Rose?

They spent the remainder of the day filling out forms, making statements, and drinking bad coffee at the police station. It was after five by the time the sheriff and his chief deputy decided they had enough information from the ladies and they could leave. But they were warned not to go far.

"Where does he think we're going to go?" Kelly asked, blinking as they stepped from the station.

"The diner?" Dottie Faye asked.

"No, I mean … Oh, never mind." Kelly shook her head.

Emma adjusted her purse strap and pointed to Dottie Faye's Cadillac parked to one side of the flat brick building. "There's the car."

They were all thankful that someone had brought Dottie

Faye's Caddy back into town and they didn't have to get a ride out to the Lapp farm to get it.

Dottie Faye unlocked the doors and slid behind the wheel, immediately adjusting the seat and mirrors. "Honestly, what did he think we were going to do? We could have driven the car back ourselves. But no. That wasn't good enough. Had to haul us in like common criminals." She finished her tirade and adjustments, then started the engine and backed out of the space. "And that sandwich for lunch." She made a face.

Emma had to agree with her on that one. "It'll be good to get a decent meal." But talk of food made her think of Hannah. *What would she eat tonight?*

"Casey said the Amish take care of themselves," Kelly recounted.

It seemed Emma wasn't the only one with Hannah on her mind. "I remember her saying that."

"I don't suppose they would take care of her bail money," Kelly mused.

Dottie Faye braked at the stoplight. "Of course not."

"The bond for murder will probably be so high they won't be able to raise it," Emma added.

"Which means she's going to be in jail for a long time," Kelly continued.

"Long, long time," Dottie Faye agreed.

"Unless the sheriff decides not to charge her," Emma mused.

Dottie Faye and Kelly both shot Emma the same weren't-you-paying-attention-back-there glare.

"Right," she said. He may not have officially arrested her, but it wouldn't be long before the sheriff threw the book at Hannah, so to speak. Emma couldn't help but feel responsible. She had been the one to insist Alvin had been murdered.

Emma had gone out there believing Hannah was innocent

of Rose's murder, but now doubt had been cast.

If it hadn't been for Emma, Hannah would be walking around, a free woman. But would her freedom be a good thing or bad?

They hadn't been in the diner more than fifteen minutes when Casey burst in. It was dinnertime, and she knew just where to find them. "Did you hear?" she asked rushing up to their table. Her cheeks were pink, her breathing erratic as if she had run all the way there.

"Sugar, we were there," Dottie Faye said.

Casey collapsed into the booth next to Kelly. "You were?" Her blue eyes grew wide. "Did you see him?"

Emma shuddered at the thought of Alvin lying on the front porch and her stepping over his prone form to get into the house.

"I suppose that means yes." She shook her head, and the untied strings attached to her cap brushed against her shoulders. "It is so sad. Did they really take Hannah Lapp to jail?"

"Yep." Dottie Faye pressed her lips together and nodded matter-of-factly.

Casey clamped a hand over her mouth in dismay. "I am worried about her. I mean, I do not know her that well, but I hate the thought of any Plain Person being in jail."

"What about being dead?"

"Dottie Faye!" Emma and Kelly said at the same time.

She shrugged. "It seems to me being dead is a little more tragic than going to jail."

Emma couldn't very well argue with that.

Kelly slumped in her seat and sighed. "I just wish she had told you who Rose was with that night."

"You and me both," Emma countered.

"Can you not ask her?" Casey looked from one of them to the other.

"She's in jail, sweetie," Dottie Faye said, drawing out each syllable as if she were speaking to a small child.

"But we could visit her." Kelly sat up a little straighter.

"Do you think the sheriff would let us see her?" Emma asked.

Dottie Faye smiled. "Only one way to find out."

All thoughts of food forgotten, Emma dropped money for their half-eaten meal onto the table and started toward the door.

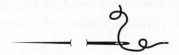

The inside of the jail smelled as if pine cleaner had been used liberally to cover the baser smells. The sheriff had refused to let them in the evening before, making them wait until visiting hours the following day.

"I hope Hannah made it through the night OK." Dottie Faye said the words, but they seemed to echo everyone's thoughts.

Emma shuddered as she caught a glimpse of the gray-painted, iron-bar cells where the prisoners were kept. Something in her gut told her Hannah would never survive long in a place like this.

A young deputy led them into a room with cinder-block walls painted a sickly shade of peach. A table sat in the center of the small room, surrounded by four plastic chairs in mismatched colors.

"She'll come through that door right there." The deputy pointed to the opposite side of the room toward a green metal door. "Keep in mind, there are cameras in here. We're watching you. So no funny business."

"Of course not." Dottie Faye puffed up as if she were offended, but fortunately she said no more.

The deputy gave them a stink-eye glare, then let himself out.

"Do you suppose this is one of those interrogation rooms?" Dottie Faye looked all around. Not that there was much to look at.

"Maybe." Kelly propped her elbows on the table and rested her chin in her hands.

"I know I'd tell them whatever they wanted to know to get out of here." Emma did her own inventory of the space, which took all of three seconds.

She turned as the door behind her opened. Hannah stepped hesitantly into the room, her hands cuffed in front of her. She looked both ways, as if she were about to step onto a busy street.

The night in jail didn't seem to have done her much harm. She wasn't beat-up or dirty, though she was missing the white cap and black bonnet she had been wearing the day before.

"Why are you here?" There was no malice in her voice, only confusion.

"Come sit down," Emma said, unsure of how to start the conversation.

Hannah chewed her lip as she mulled over the idea.

"We didn't come here to hurt you," Kelly said softly.

She remained standing. "Why were you at my house yesterday?"

"We needed to talk to you some more about Rose."

"So you came to my house?"

They nodded.

Hannah ducked her head. Without her Amish cap in place, Emma could make out a few strands of gray in the honey-blond tresses. "She was lucky then. To have friends like you."

"Rose?" Emma asked around the lump forming in her throat.

"*Jah.*" As if sensing they meant her no harm, Hannah completed the few steps she needed to reach the chair. She slid into it, the handcuffs around her wrists clanking against the tabletop.

She seemed smaller somehow, as if the steel cuffs had diminished her size, or maybe it was her soul. She looked so defeated.

"I'm sorry about your husband." Dottie Faye covered one of Hannah's hands with her own.

That was the thing about her aunt. She could be crazy and over the top, a little unorthodox and a lot loud, but she was caring straight through to her core.

Hannah shrugged. "He didn't love me anymore, but ..." Her voice hitched. "I never wanted him dead." She pulled herself together, tamping back the tears that thickened her tone. "The worst part is, I can't even pray."

"There, there," Dottie Faye soothed, patting Hannah's hand. "You just tell God whatever you feel in your heart. He's listening."

Hannah shook her head. "I cannot pray without my *kapp*. A woman's hair must be covered in reverence. The deputy took my prayer *kapp*."

Emma caught Dottie Faye's gaze from across the table.

Her aunt shrugged.

"I'm sure He would understand this one time," Kelly murmured.

Hannah pulled herself together. "What did you want to ask me?"

The women stared at her.

"About Rose?" Hannah prompted.

"O-oh," Emma stuttered. "You said you saw Rose at a pub the night before she died."

Hannah nodded.

"With a student?"

"*Jah*."

"Who?" Emma asked.

Hannah shook her head. "I do not remember his name."

"So, it was a man?" Kelly asked.

"Oh, *jah*."

"Did you talk to her that night?" Emma continued.

"*Nay*." Hannah ducked her head. "They were …" She cleared her throat. "They seemed like they didn't want to be disturbed. You know, intimate."

Rose with a student? This was the first she had heard about anything like that. Emma swung her gaze to Kelly.

Kelly shook her head.

"You don't remember who he was." Emma's words didn't quite form a question. "Do you remember what he looked like?"

"*Nay*. I am sorry. It has been a very long time."

"Well, now you have a new suspect." Dottie Faye dug in her purse and pulled out her spy-cam sunglasses.

"Don't you dare turn those on in here," Emma warned, her voice low.

Her aunt pouted.

Hannah looked from one of them to the other. "Did you come here, to New York, because you thought I had something to do with Rose's murder?"

"We, uh, thought you might have some information that could help us."

"What sort of information? Like what I just told you? That is all I know."

"What about a DNA sample? We need one of those." Dottie Faye placed the sunglasses on the top of her head, but didn't turn them on.

"A DNA sample?" Hannah's brow puckered in confusion.

"You know." Dottie Faye patted her hand. "Genetic codes and such."

Hannah moved her hands away from Dottie Faye's grasp.

"It's just as important that we clear all the suspects as it is we find the killer," Emma said. "Do you understand?"

"So you need my DNA?" Her blue eyes were steady as she waited for the answer.

"Yes, if you're willing to do that," Emma said.

"I am already a suspect in one murder; I do not wish to have to defend myself in two."

"A strand of hair would work fine," Kelly put in.

Hannah reached up and pulled a hair from her head as easy as that. She held it toward Kelly. "Where are you getting the suspects?"

"From the quilt you students made in class," Emma answered as Kelly found an envelope in her purse and carefully placed the hair inside.

Recognition lit Hannah's features. "Oh, I forgot about that."

As ugly as it was, Emma couldn't blame her. "Everyone wrote their name on the back of their own block."

"You have all these names?"

"We have the quilt blocks," Kelly said.

"Not with us," Emma clarified.

Hannah looked disappointed. "I might be able to remember if I could see names." She shifted in her chair, the handcuffs clanking once again. She looked down at them ruefully, then raised her gaze to Emma. "Now that I have helped you, will you help me in return?"

"Of course." Emma was surprised at how easily the words slipped from her lips.

"There is a boy—Matthew Lapp—who takes care of the

horses with Alvin. He should be at the farm this afternoon. He usually comes about three." A frown puckered her brow. "At least I hope he will still show up. Will you meet him out there and tell him to keep taking care of the animals?"

"You bet we will," Dottie Faye reassured her.

"It would mean a lot to me. I don't have anyone else to help me."

Emma tried not to register how sad and hopeless the words sounded as they fell from Hannah's lips.

"You can count on us," Kelly added.

"*Danki*," Hannah murmured. "He will need to come as long as I am in jail." She tried to smile, but it looked more like she had stomach pain instead of hope.

"Now, don't you worry none about that either." Dottie Faye patted her on the shoulder. "We'll get you out of here just as fast as we can."

Emma was still shaking her head over her aunt's promise to Hannah as they exited the jailhouse.

"Now what do we do?" Kelly asked.

"We get some bail money for that poor girl. Bless her heart," Dottie Faye purred.

"Aunt Dottie, we can't bail her out of jail."

Dottie Faye frowned at Emma's slip. "I don't see why not."

"Well, first there's the fact that no bond has been set, and if bond is set, it will be astronomical. We're just going to have to wait until the sheriff has no choice but to release her."

"You can't believe that innocent child is guilty," Dottie Faye said.

"Why are you so sure she isn't?" Emma asked.

Dottie Faye crossed her arms. "I can see it in her eyes."

Emma opened her mouth to protest further, but Kelly grabbed her elbow. "Look there." She pointed to the parking lot. Two rows down from Dottie Faye's Cadillac was a sleek silver Mercedes.

"That looks like the one—"

"—that almost ran us off the road."

"What's it doing here?" Emma asked.

Kelly shook her head.

Dottie Faye did an about-face and started back toward the station. "I don't know, but I'm about to find out."

twelve

Emma raced behind her aunt, doing her best to catch up. How the woman could walk so fast in heels would forever remain a mystery. She got to the front counter of the sheriff's office two steps after her aunt demanded to know who the "fancy-shmancy Mercedes" in the parking lot belonged to.

The uniformed woman behind the counter blinked as if trying to bring such brazen pluck into focus, then coughed. "The sheriff's mother. Why?"

Dottie Faye deflated like a leaky balloon. "No reason," she mumbled.

"Come on," Emma hissed. "You're going to get us arrested."

"What's going on out here?" The sheriff came out of his office, a tiny, white-haired lady on his arm. His mother.

"These ladies wanted to know—"

"Nothing," Kelly interjected. "We're fine, really."

"Just leaving," Emma added.

They backed toward the door while the sheriff frowned. His mother watched, perplexed, and the dispatch officer's mouth hung open.

Thankfully they made it out into the sunshine without anyone calling them back.

"That was close," Emma breathed.

"Pshaw." Dottie Faye waved one hand as if wiping away her niece's concern.

"I didn't get a good look at who was driving the car," Kelly said. "But I'm fairly certain it wasn't the sheriff's mother."

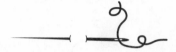

"Do you really think the charge will stick?" Kelly asked as they gathered around the tiny café-style table in the common area. Tea had been served, and the trio settled in to decide what to do next.

After their close brush with the sheriff, they immediately went to the post office to overnight the hair sample to their contact at the lab. Now all they could do was wait.

"If the sheriff wants it to, it will." Emma took a sip of her coffee. "Kelly, I think we should call your mother and have her send us the quilt blocks."

"That's a great idea," Kelly said. "Maybe if Hannah sees them, she'll remember who Rose was with that night. With all the names on the back of each square, surely one will ring a bell. In fact, there are only two male students left."

"We've got two days before we hear back from the lab." Two more days in New York. Two days that would lead them closer to the truth about Rose's death.

"Don't forget you promised to help Hannah," Dottie Faye reminded them.

"Well, *you* promised we'd help her," Emma said. "And I'm not sure what we can do."

"Nothing for another forty-eight hours." Kelly peeled the crust off her banana bread and started picking the nuts out of the slice. "Hopefully by then, the sheriff will realize how ridiculous it is to charge Hannah with murder, and he'll be forced to set her free."

"I don't like it." Dottie Faye harrumphed.

"Honestly, jail is the safest place for her right now," Kelly said.

Emma agreed. "Whoever killed Alvin might decide to come after her next."

"So you think she's innocent?" Dottie Faye pressed.

"We're not taking any chances until we know for sure."

"Two days," Dottie Faye warned. "Two days, and then we're busting her out."

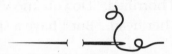

The drive out to the Lapp farm seemed shorter this trip. Maybe because they didn't pass a multitude of buggies, and no one tried to run them off the road. Or maybe because the lack of urgency allowed them to enjoy the pastoral scene as they rolled through the lush country.

"Do you ever wonder why she left here?" Kelly asked as they neared the farm.

Emma swung the car into the drive, barely missing the rut off to the left. "Sure, and then I wonder why she came back."

"It does have a certain charm." Kelly unhooked her seat belt and slid from the car.

Dottie Faye did the same, a look of disbelief on her face. "It has something." She gazed around the dilapidated farm. "But I'm not sure I would call it charm."

Emma shut her car door and pointed toward the ducks and hens pecking around in the sparse grass that made up the front yard. "Do you think we should feed them?"

Kelly shrugged. "That may be one of Alvin's helper's duties." She came around the front of the car. Emma couldn't help but notice that like her, Kelly had a hard time looking at the house. The crime scene tape still wrapped around the porch posts—a big X that warned anyone from entering the house.

"What about her cat?" Dottie Faye asked.

As if sensing that someone was talking about her, the cat sauntered around the side of the house. She made her way over to the car and meowed at the trio of women watching her.

"What do we do if the helper doesn't show?" Kelly asked.

"I suppose we feed the horses," Emma replied.

Dottie looked horrified. "Do you know how to do that?"

Emma shook her head. "But I have a smartphone. I can look it up."

"How hard can it be?" Kelly asked.

But Emma was saved from having to answer as a horse and buggy pulled into the drive.

A young man, no more than fourteen or fifteen, hopped down from the driver's seat and looked at the three English women standing in the yard.

"Hi." He nodded to each one of them in turn. If he was surprised to find them there, he never showed it. "I am Matthew Lapp."

"Hi, Matthew. We're, uh ... friends of Hannah's." Emma's words almost sounded convincing. "She wanted us to come out here and let you know that she still needs you to come feed the horses while she's, uh ..." She fluttered one hand around unable to complete the sentence.

"*Jah*," he said. "OK." Then he tilted his head at a thoughtful angle. "Did she think I would not come?"

"I think she was worried, yes," Emma replied.

"Tell her not to worry." He gave them a nod, then started to unhitch his horse from the buggy. "I will come every day until she is home."

"Good, good." Emma nodded her head, feeling like a dashboard ornament.

"Who's that?" Dottie Faye turned as a red pickup truck

pulled into the drive. It stopped, then backed out and headed off in the same direction from which it had come.

"That was weird," Kelly muttered.

"Too much of a coincidence," Dottie Faye said with a quick nod.

"What?" Emma asked.

"We passed a truck just like that coming out here the other day. Not just the silver Mercedes at all." Dottie Faye hustled around the car as the young Matthew Lapp watched in awe. "Let's go."

"Go where?" Emma asked.

"After him, after him." Dottie Faye slid into the driver's seat. "That could be our killer."

"Are you serious?" Emma propped her hands on her hips.

"Of course I am."

"Kelly?" Emma turned to her friend.

But Kelly had already slid into the shotgun seat, always one to egg on Dottie Faye and her cockamamy ideas.

"Oh, for heaven's sake," Emma grumbled. She turned to the teen. "Will you feed the cat and the ducks?"

"*Jah*," he said. "And the chickens too."

Dottie Faye revved the engine. "They're getting away."

"Tell Hannah Lapp that I will take care of it all," he said. "She has my word."

It was the best anyone could ask for. "Thanks." She slid into the car and waved to the boy, then Dottie Faye sped down the country road.

"Now, where did they go?" Dottie Faye scooted up in the seat peering over the steering wheel as if she was driving in pouring rain.

"There." Kelly pointed to the left. A cloud of dust trailed behind the red pickup that had just turned.

"We're on 'em now." Dottie Faye smiled with glee, but never took her eyes from the road.

"Don't let them get away," Kelly said.

"Don't encourage her." Emma frowned at her best friend. One of them had to be the voice of reason.

"Come on, Emma. This is the most fun we've had since we've been here."

Emma couldn't argue with that. "OK, but don't follow too close," she said instead.

"Is the passenger wearing a cowboy hat?" Dottie Faye leaned over the steering wheel to get a better look. She eased her foot down a little harder on the gas, closing some of the distance between the two vehicles.

"He's got on *some* kind of hat," Kelly said.

"I knew it." Dottie Faye pounded one hand against the steering wheel.

The truck in front of them sped up.

Dottie Faye pressed the gas a bit harder to keep up. "Why is he driving so fast?"

"Do you think he spotted us?" Kelly said.

"Really? This car's not exactly inconspicuous," Emma said.

"Good point," Dottie Faye said. "Maybe I should drop back a little more."

Too late. The driver slammed on his brakes, sending the truck skidding on two tires.

It came to rest across the middle of the road so they couldn't pass.

Dottie Faye braked hard and managed to keep the Caddy facing in the right direction without T-boning into the side of the truck.

"What are you doing?" A young man no more than twenty hopped down from the cab. He stormed back to where they waited in the car. He was dressed in Amish clothes, though he was clean-shaven, not bearded like the other men they had seen. His suspenders were missing and his shirt was untucked.

"Uh-oh," Kelly said with a grimace. "Road rage."

"Pray he doesn't have a gun," Dottie Faye said out of one corner of her mouth. She got out of the car and drew herself to her full height. With the aid of her nosebleed heels, she topped the young man by several inches. "What business do you have at the Lapp farm?" she demanded.

He stopped, obviously confused. Or was that just an act? "We were turning around."

A young girl slid from the other side of the vehicle. She was dressed in hip-hugging jeans and a New York Mets T-shirt. She wore a hat like the Amish favored over her long blond hair. His hat?

"Did my dad hire you?"

"I think we have a case of mistaken identity," Emma said, sliding from the car to stand next to her aunt.

Kelly also got out. There was power in numbers.

"You were not following us?"

"Oh, we were," Dottie Faye said.

Emma wanted to kick her. "What my aunt means is we were following you because we thought you were someone else."

The young man's brows knit together. "You aren't here to stop us?"

"From what?" Dottie Faye asked.

"No," Emma said. "We're sorry to have bothered you."

"Jacob, let's go." The girl looped her arm through his and tugged him back toward the truck. They both slid in through the driver's-side door. In an instant, they were gone.

"Do you think ...?" Dottie Faye turned to Emma as they went back to their own car.

She nodded. "Yes. I think you may have just crashed someone's elopement."

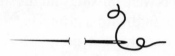

The next day was perhaps the most boring of Emma's life. Waiting around for something to happen was not on her list of fun things to do. They hung around the B&B, checked the mail, went to the quilt shop, and ate. Not the most productive day of her life, but after nearly being run off the road, finding a dead body, and chasing down a couple of love-struck kids, she was ready for a little downtime.

"Do you think the person in the silver Mercedes killed Alvin?" Dottie Faye asked as they waited for their package. The common area was deserted except for them, and that was just fine with Emma. Surely the quilt would be delivered today.

She shrugged. "We passed two buggies that day as well. Maybe it was one of them."

"And the red truck," Dottie Faye chirped. "Don't forget the red truck."

"I don't remember a truck," Emma countered.

"Well, I do."

"You think the murderer is Amish?" Kelly asked.

"I didn't say that. Though it's possible."

"Anything is possible," Dottie Faye added.

Kelly nodded and knitted her brow, seeming to mull it over.

"The man in the cowboy hat," Dottie Faye interjected. "I think he was in one of the buggies."

"Or an Amish man in a hat," Emma countered. "Or even an English girl in an Amish man's hat, like yesterday."

"Well, shoot." Dottie Faye sat back and sighed. "We're no farther along than we were two days ago."

The bell above the door jingled. They all glanced up to see who was coming in.

The overnight carrier.

Dottie Faye rose and knocked over her chair in her haste. "Is that for Emma Cotton?" She righted her chair and hurried to stand in front of him.

He squinted at the address. "Kelly Grace."

"That's me." Kelly made her way over and signed the electronic pad.

"The quilt blocks," Emma said.

Kelly set the package on the table.

Dottie Faye dug in her purse and brought out a pair of scissors.

"Where'd you—" Emma shook her head. "Never mind."

Carefully, Kelly cut the box open and removed the tissue-wrapped blocks.

"Do you think the sheriff will let us in to see her again?"

Dottie Faye *tsked*. "That poor girl. I can't believe she's been in jail three whole days."

Emma didn't bother to point out that it had been less than forty-eight hours over the span of three days. Dottie Faye had planted herself firmly in Hannah's camp, and there was no benefit in debating the semantics.

"There's only one way to find out," Kelly said.

Emma and Kelly grabbed their purses while Dottie Faye settled herself down in her seat.

"You aren't coming with us?" Kelly asked.

She shook her head. "I think I'll stay here and wait for any more packages."

Emma nodded. "Sounds like a great plan."

Dottie Faye handed them the keys to the Caddy, and the girls headed out.

The uniformed dispatch officer gave them a stern frown as they entered the police station, but the sheriff granted their request to meet with Hannah.

After a deputy checked the box with the quilt blocks, they were led into the same room where they had waited for her previously.

"I hope this works," Kelly said, sliding into one of the hard plastic chairs.

"You and me both." Emma sat down beside her and unwrapped the quilt blocks.

It was a mess now that it had been taken apart, but it held the key to finding out who had pushed Rose down those stairs fifteen years ago.

Hannah entered the room looking more tired and run-down than she had the last time they were there.

"Hi, Hannah."

Hannah eased into the chair and cast a smile in Emma's direction. "Is that the quilt?"

"Yes." Emma unfolded the blocks from the tissue paper, carefully spreading them out so Hannah could see.

She squinted at the names, running her fingers over the stitches as she examined each and every one of them. She shook her head. "I'm sorry, but I don't remember."

Emma exhaled, only then realizing that she had held her breath while Hannah studied the names on the quilt. Maybe if they showed her some pictures of her long-ago classmates ....

"Are you going to help me?" Hannah asked, her voice timid and soft.

"We said we would." Emma didn't want to tell her that

they were waiting on the results of the DNA test. That was something the woman didn't need to know.

"We went out to the farm and talked to Matthew. He said he would handle everything."

"He's a *gut* boy, that Matthew Lapp." Hannah tried to smile once again, this time no more successful than the first. "I can't sleep here. Every time I close my eyes, I see Alvin's face."

"We're working on it," Kelly said. She picked up the blocks and tucked them back into the tissue paper.

"I'm sorry I couldn't be more help." Hannah stood and shuffled back to the door she had entered from. Her shoulders were slumped; she looked thoroughly beaten.

Then Emma realized that while Alvin may not have loved Hannah, and they might have even had a terrible relationship, he was all she had had. And now he was gone.

They left the room, and the waiting officer escorted them down the long hallway.

"Immediately," a familiar voice said as they made their way toward the front of the sheriff's office.

"Is that Dottie Faye?" Kelly asked.

Emma frowned. "It sounded like her."

They quickened their pace.

"That means *now*," the voice continued.

"Yep," Emma said. "That's her."

They rounded the corner to see Dottie Faye, hands braced on her hips as she stared down the dispatch officer. The woman was on the phone, looking harried instead of intimidating as she had when they arrived. Dottie Faye had her usual bluster of Southern hurricane.

"Dottie Faye, what are you doing here?" Emma asked.

"I've come to get Hannah Lapp out of jail."

"We've already talked about this," Emma reminded her.

"Yes, we did.While you were gone, we got the results of the DNA test. Hannah didn't murder Rose. And she didn't murder Alvin either."

Emma took her aunt by the arm and led her away from the desk. "We've been over this," she said, her voice as patient as she could muster. "After seventy-two hours, the sheriff has to charge her or set her free."

"What if he charges her?"

"Then we plead her case. But until tomorrow afternoon, she has to stay put, like it or not."

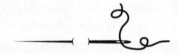

The following afternoon, they waited in the foyer for the officers to bring Hannah out to them. The sheriff could find no evidence against Hannah and had been advised by the district attorney to free her until such evidence could be found.

She came hesitantly, peering around the corner as if she wasn't sure what she would find on the other side.

Her cap was back on her head, and she wore the apron she'd had on when they arrested her. Emma hadn't noticed it was missing until she saw it again. Both garments were made out of the same heavy gray fabric.

"You did it," Hannah said as if she wasn't accustomed to people keeping their word. Emma supposed that with a husband like Alvin Lapp, Hannah was probably well versed in the art of handling disappointment. "You helped me."

"You're not in the clear yet," Emma told her. "But you're free to go home for now." She didn't bother to tell Hannah that the sheriff was frantically trying to dig up evidence to formally charge her with Alvin's murder. Some things were better left unsaid.

Hannah blanched and shook her head. "I can't go back there."

"Of course not," Dottie Faye drawled.

"I could stay with my mother-in-law, I suppose." But her voice sounded anything but hopeful.

"That woman we saw you with at the mercantile?" Dottie Faye pulled a face.

"She's the only kin I have left."

Dottie Faye smiled. "Well, sugar, now you have us."

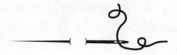

Mrs. Yoder seemed none too happy that Hannah was moving in, but the suite could handle four, so she had to agree.

"Maybe tomorrow we can drive out to your house and pick up some clean clothes for you."

"I'll just wash this out for tonight." Hannah plucked at her dress.

Emma loaned her a pair of yoga pants and a T-shirt to wear around the suite while her dress dripped dry over the bathtub.

"This feels sinful." Hannah ran her hands down the legs of the pants as she sat on the sofa.

"Pah." Dottie Faye waved away her concern. "It's like a girls' night. Do you ever have those?"

"We have sisters' day. That's when a group of women get together and can vegetables or make jelly."

"But you wore pants on your run-around time. What do you call it?"

"*Rumspringa,*" Hannah supplied.

"Rum-spring-ah," Kelly repeated.

"I wore jeans sometimes under my dress, but I never wore pants out. Even though I was away from home, I couldn't shake the habit of wearing a dress."

"I can understand that," Emma said.

Hannah picked at the fabric on the heather gray pants. "I'm not looking forward to going back to the house tomorrow."

"Oh, sugar, he's not there any longer."

"I know, but ...." She shrugged. "I just can't believe the sheriff thinks I poisoned the pie."

"Would he have any reason to think that? Other than the fact that yours and Alvin's relationship was rocky?"

A frown puckered her brow. "I do not understand what you say, but there is one thing." She took a deep breath. "I'm known for my cherry pies."

"We heard," Kelly said.

"But I didn't make the pie that Alvin was eating when he ...." She stopped. "See, Alvin didn't really like cherry pie, so I never made it for him. His favorite was strawberry-rhubarb. But he didn't like mine as much as his *mudder's*."

"Typical male." Dottie Faye rolled her eyes.

"This was definitely a cherry pie," Emma said. "I may not know much about pies, but that was obvious."

"I saw it." Hannah said. "Ben Lambright made it."

Ben Lambright. Emma had heard that name somewhere before. "The baker?"

"*Jah.*"

"You're sure about that?"

Hannah nodded. "He has a special way of crimping his pie crust. Did you see how it looked—"

"Braided," Kelly supplied. "I noticed that."

"Ben Lambright does that to all his pies. No one else in the settlement does that."

"But that means ..." Kelly started, then turned her gaze to Emma.

The argument they had witnessed replayed itself in Emma's mind. "There was no love lost between Ben and Alvin," she said.

But did the baker hold a big enough grudge to kill Alvin Lapp?

thirteen

"Do you really think Ben Lambright could be responsible for Alvin's death?" Hannah asked over breakfast the following morning. Her dress was dry and clean, her prayer cap pinned to her hair. She looked more Amish than they had seen her in a while.

"Honey, anyone could be." Dottie Faye pointed her fork at Hannah. "But don't you worry now. These girls are on the case."

Emma started to protest. Maybe she was on the case. She had promised Hannah she would help. What else did she have to do until Hannah remembered the student she had seen with Rose the night before she died? What else indeed?

Besides, Hannah couldn't rely on the sheriff's office to help her. They already had their man, so to speak. Plus, Emma had seen enough cop shows to know the value of the first forty-eight hours in a case. They were a day past that, and time was ticking.

"What if we head over to the bakery and see if we can talk to Ben?" Kelly suggested.

Hannah looked a little frightened by the idea. Maybe it wasn't the bakery as much as leaving the B&B. While they had been eating, she had garnered several odd looks from staff and guests alike. Emma supposed in a town the size Fort Plain, word got around quickly.

"That's a great idea." Dottie Faye stood and slung her purse strap over her shoulder. "Maybe we can get to the bottom of this today."

Emma had no illusions that the mystery of who killed Alvin Lapp could be solved with a morning's work, but the bakery was the best place to start.

The place was hopping when they arrived. English and Amish alike stood in line to buy bread and other pastries. A side counter had been set up as a coffee station, and a few tables and chairs had been added for those who wanted to sit for a time.

Dottie Faye joined the crush waiting in line while Emma, Hannah, and Kelly found an empty table to claim. Luckily, most of the customers were on their way to work and were hustling out the door with their purchases, not waiting around any longer than they had to.

Ben Lambright stood behind the counter taking orders while a young Amish girl rang them into the cash register. For a moment Emma wondered how the device worked, but then she realized that the bakery had electricity. They did, however, use a wood-burning oven to bake their treats.

A few minutes later, Dottie Faye returned to the table carrying a tray.

"You bought the whole pie?" Emma asked.

Dottie Faye shrugged and set the tray on the table. "That way we each can try it."

"Well, that's not suspicious at all," Kelly quipped.

"I'm not sure how tasting the pie is going to help us." Emma eyed the pie with distrust. Ben Lambright appeared to be an upstanding member of the community. He might have killed Alvin Lapp, but that didn't mean that he poisoned every cherry pie he made. Still ....

Dottie Faye took the plastic knife and started hacking into the pie. Emma had to admit it looked good. More than that, it was the prettiest pie she had ever seen. No wonder the B&B bought his pies to serve during their teas.

Her aunt doled out portions using a fork and the edge of the knife. *"Bon appétit."* She scooped up a bite, but didn't manage to lift it all the way to her mouth. "You don't think ...?"

"Oh, no, no."

Hannah, Kelly, and Emma all shook their heads, but no one could actually eat the pie.

"Did he know who you were?" Emma asked.

"I don't think so." Dottie Faye stared at the pie as if it might explode any minute.

"He'll figure it out soon enough." Kelly nodded toward Ben. He'd caught sight of them, his eyes narrowed as if in deep thought.

Emma turned her attention back to her plate. The pie did look delicious.

"Guder mariye." Ben smiled in greeting as he wiped his hands on a small towel.

"Hello." Emma placed her fork by her plate, grateful to have an excuse not to eat.

"What does that mean?" Dottie Faye loudly asked.

"It means 'Good morning,'" he explained. Then he turned his attention to Hannah. "Hannah Lapp, I came to offer my sympathies to you. If there is anything I can do to help you in this time of need ...."

She ducked her head over her plate, but didn't immediately respond. *"Danki,* Ben Lambright."

"You are friends of Hannah's?" he asked, looking around the table.

Emma nodded and introduced everyone.

"Why do you have electricity and the mercantile doesn't?" Leave it to Dottie Faye to move things right along.

Ben smiled. "We're not in the same church district. His

bishop does not allow them to use electricity for any reason. My bishop allows it for my business only."

Kelly's face pulled into a frown of confusion. "But you're both Amish."

"It is complicated," Ben said.

"Did you kill Alvin Lapp?" Dottie Faye blurted, taking them all by surprise.

Emma kicked her under the table. "That's not what my aunt meant to say."

"It was too." She shot Emma a stern look, then reached down to rub her leg.

"Why would I kill Alvin Lapp?" Ben asked.

"Are you aware that one of your pies may have been used to poison him?" Dottie Faye sounded like a DA in cross-examination mode.

Ben grew pale. "I did not know." He shook his head. "I sell pies all day. Many of them."

"It was your pie all right," Dottie Faye added.

"I would never harm Alvin Lapp. Or anyone else."

"We were there," Kelly said. "We saw the confrontation between the two of you at the B&B."

"One disagreement spawns a murder? No, Kelly Grace. I am a peaceful man."

Dottie Faye shook her head. "That argument didn't look peaceful to me."

Ben heaved a sigh. "*Ach*," he said, and Dottie Faye leaned closer to him as if to get the juiciest details first. "I do not like the way Alvin Lapp treats his *fraa*. His wife," he explained.

"Treated," Kelly said. "He's dead, remember?"

Ben nodded. "I remember."

"Go on," Emma said.

"That is all." Ben clasped his hands together on top of the

table. "I stopped getting eggs from him. I talked to my bishop in hopes that he and Alvin's bishop might work something out between them."

"I guess that didn't happen?" Emma asked.

Hannah shook her head. "I appreciate that," she said to Ben. "That you took the time to try and help. Alvin loved me," she added, her tone stronger than Emma could have imagined. "In his own way, he always did."

Dottie Faye frowned, not her normal expression. "Why did you care how he treated her?"

"She is my cousin," he explained.

"Really?" she asked Hannah.

She nodded. "Very distant."

"But a cousin all the same," Ben added. "Hannah deserves someone who can care for her and take care of her proper."

No wonder Ben had boycotted Alvin's eggs. Too bad more people in the community hadn't followed his example.

"I did not like how he treated her, but I would never go as far as to hurt the man. Alvin has been very angry with me for ending our business together. It would make more sense if he had tried to kill me instead of the other way around."

Emma couldn't argue with that logic, and something in Ben's tone made it seem like he thought Alvin was more than capable of murder.

She shivered.

"I must get back to work. We are shorthanded these days. Enjoy your pie," Ben said. Then he went back behind the counter to help take care of the rest of his customers.

"It was not all bad, you know." Hannah's voice was quiet but steady. "Being married to Alvin, I mean." She sounded as if she wasn't accustomed to talking about relationship matters.

Was that something else the Amish didn't do that the English did?

"He tried," she continued. "But some heartaches never heal."

Emma felt terrible for Hannah. If she hadn't been Amish, she would have taken her out to eat, drink wine, maybe get a mani-pedi and some ice cream, but as it was ....

"We should go out and do something tonight," Kelly said, almost reading Emma's mind.

"In this town?" Dottie Faye looked out the window.

She was right. Fort Plain was about as unexciting as they came, but Emma wanted to do something that would distract Hannah, if only for a few hours. Something more than just help her find out who murdered her husband. "We'll think of something."

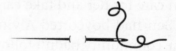

"Why did you come get me from jail?" Hannah sat on the couch in the living area of their suite. She had removed her shoes and tucked her feet beneath her on the couch. Every so often, she would run a hand over the soft fabric of the couch.

Emma remembered the hard wooden bench that sat in the living room at Hannah and Alvin's. Were all their couches like that?

"Because we know you're innocent," Dottie Faye answered.

"Of killing Alvin?" she asked.

"Of killing Rose."

Hannah's mouth formed a small O. "You also believe Rose was murdered?"

Emma nodded. "We do. But the police won't listen."

"So you are trying to find out who killed her on your own? Like that show, *Murder, She Wrote*?"

Kelly laughed. "Something like that."

"How do you know about a television show?" Emma asked.

"My *rumspringa*."

"Hannah, why did you come back here?"

She ran her hands down her skirt where it covered her knees. "It is hard being in the English world when you are Amish. Things are different. Nothing in our upbringing prepares us for the reality that is out there."

"OK, that I can believe," Dottie Faye said. "But why did you marry a man you didn't love?"

Hannah sighed. "Amish don't always marry for love. There are other things that are important too."

"Like what?" Emma asked.

"Family. Ability to provide. Community standing."

The sight of the Lapp house with its peeling paint and dilapidated porch flashed in her mind's eye. She looked to Kelly and knew they were thinking the same thing.

"I did love him once," Hannah continued, almost as if she were aware that her words weren't exactly the truth. "And he loved me, but love is not always enough."

Kelly punched a few more keys on the computer and took it over to Hannah. The woman straightened and put her feet on the plush rug that sat beneath the couch.

"Here's the school website. There are a few pictures here to help. Maybe you can spot the student Rose was talking to that night."

Hannah nodded and accepted the laptop. "What if I do not see him?"

"Then we keep looking," Emma said simply.

"You care about her that much?" Hannah asked.

"I do," Emma said.

Hannah ducked her head and started tumbling through the pictures. "I wish I had a friend like you."

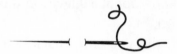

"Why didn't you and Alvin have children?"

They were seated in the diner, chatting over plates of cheeseburgers and fries. Comfort food at its finest.

"Dottie Faye, really," Emma admonished. "That's too personal. Hannah, you don't have to answer that."

Hannah ducked her head over her meal then raised her chin with a renewed strength that Emma didn't know she possessed. *She'll be all right,* Emma thought. *Maybe not today or the next, but soon.*

"I do not know, really. It just never happened for us. Though ... though Alvin said it was God's way of punishing me for leaving the community after I had joined the church."

Kelly gasped.

"That was a terrible thing to say!" Dottie Faye exclaimed.

Emma agreed.

"It is *allrecht,*" Hannah said. "I know that he was afraid he was the problem. The reason we ... uh, you know." She turned bright pink and took a big gulp of her soda.

"You're not used to talking about such matters are you, sugar?" Dottie Faye patted her hand.

Hannah shook her head.

"Were you embarrassed when you saw Rose with the student that night?" Emma asked. "Is that why you're having such a hard time remembering who it was?"

"*Jah,* I think so." She raised her gaze to look at them, her backbone strengthening once again. "I did not want to pry, and I had never gotten used to seeing people sit so close."

"Are you sure it was one of your classmates? I mean, it was fifteen years ago. Maybe you're mistaken," Emma said. "It might not even have been Rose."

"*Nay*," Hannah said. "It was her."

Her tone was confident, steadfast. Emma didn't really know what Hannah had seen that night, but she certainly believed it to be Rose.

Yet the image of her friend and an unknown student cuddled up together in a bar .... Something about it just wasn't right. Rose had been her best friend. They'd shared everything. If she had a new beau, wouldn't she have told Emma?

"Do you miss it?" Dottie Faye asked. "The outside world, I mean?"

Hannah's expression took a faraway, dreamy quality, then she shook her head. "There were parts that I enjoyed. The soft furniture is one." Emma recalled the way Hannah had run her hands over the couch back at the B&B. "I miss being able to sleep in on the weekends."

"Why can't you sleep in now?" Dottie Faye asked.

"On a farm, there is always something that needs to be milked or fed."

Kelly chuckled.

"Speaking of," Emma started, "has Matthew been working with you a long time?"

"A while," she said.

"Any relation to Alvin?" Emma asked.

"Not close enough to talk about," Hannah said.

"But he doesn't work there all the time?" Emma asked.

Kelly shot her a knowing look. Could Matthew be involved in the murder?

Hannah picked up on it and shook her head. "Matthew is just fourteen. And he only comes to the house when the horses are there."

"So they really aren't yours?" Kelly asked.

"They belong to some men who live in Vernon."

"Vernon, New York?" Emma frowned. Why did that sound familiar?

"Horse racing!" Dottie Faye exclaimed in the manner of someone shouting "Eureka!" "There's a horse track there."

"*Jah*," Hannah said. "Alvin would take the horses in and train them for these men."

"Train?" Kelly asked. "Like riding?"

Emma was also incredulous. Alvin had been much too large to serve as a jockey.

Hannah shook her head. "Nay, not like that. He would just work with them. Give them exercise and such. Then when they needed them for a race, they would come and get them."

"They wouldn't happen to drive a silver Mercedes, would they?" Emma asked.

"Not to pick up the horses, *nay*." A confused frown puckered her brow.

"Have they ever come out to the house to visit or discuss business with Alvin?"

"Once or twice."

"How about then?" Kelly asked. "Did they drive a fancy silver car those times?"

Hannah thought about it for a moment. "*Jah*," she finally said. "There was one time. *Jah*, they drove a silver car, but I do not remember what a Mercedes is."

Emma's heart started to pound. It might not be a step in the right direction of finding out who had killed Rose, but it might just be the ticket to finding out who had killed Alvin Lapp.

fourteen

A silver car, perhaps the Mercedes that had nearly run Emma, Kelly, and Dottie Faye off the road the day of Alvin's murder, had visited the Lapp farm before. The only problem was, Alvin Lapp hadn't kept Hannah apprised of all of his business practices.

"You have no idea who those men were?" Emma asked. A brand-new day had dawned, and they were no closer to solving either of the murders than they had been when they started.

Emma buttered a muffin and tried not to think of all the calories it was costing her. Breakfast had been served, and the four of them were in the common room. Emma and Kelly wanted to get to the bottom of the matter with Hannah, while Dottie Faye seemed more interested in the return of the man in the cowboy hat.

"He's back," she whispered, interrupting their conversation.

Emma silently acknowledged her aunt.

"Business was not something Alvin discussed with me," Hannah said, unaware of their interest in Cowboy Hat Man.

One by one, the suspects were falling by the wayside—not that there had many to begin with. The man in the cowboy hat was looking better and better.

"The men," Kelly said. "You say they live in Vernon?"

"I suppose. The racetrack is there."

"But you're not sure where they live," Emma said.

"*Nay.*"

Kelly blew her hair out of her face, then leaned back in her chair. "We just can't catch a break."

"I know this sounds bad," Emma said, "but I was hoping that Ben Lambright was the one."

"He could still be. We haven't totally ruled him out," Kelly said.

"*Jah*," Hannah agreed.

"You got that right." Dottie Faye pulled her glasses down and stared at Cowboy Hat Man, though her words were directed at Emma.

"What do you mean?" she asked.

Dottie Faye turned her attention back to her table companions. She leaned forward, pushed her sunglasses back up, and whispered. "Ben Lambright takes Coumadin."

"Well, that's it then," Kelly said, throwing her hands in the air in mock celebration. "Case solved."

Emma shot her a look. The longer they stayed in New York, the thinner her patience wore. "What does that have to do with the case, Dottie Faye?"

"See, I went to the drugstore to get some lipstick. I think someone took mine." She raised her carefully plucked brows and shot a pointed look toward the young Amish girl refilling the scrambled eggs. "Anyway, I overheard Ben the Baker talking with the pharmacist about his prescription. Ben said he dropped part of his medication down the sink. Pretty suspicious, don't you think?"

"Well, no, Dottie Faye," Emma said as gently as she could. "Why is that suspicious?"

"Because," she said earnestly. "Coumadin is an anticoagulant."

"Yes." Kelly nodded.

"The main ingredient is warfarin sodium."

"And?" Emma gestured to Dottie Faye to speed it up.

"And that, my dears, is the main ingredient in rat poison." She sat back triumphantly, then snapped her glasses back into place, apparently realizing she was missing some good footage of the man in the cowboy hat eating toast.

Hannah gasped, her face stricken. "Rat poison?"

"How do you know these things?" Kelly asked.

Dottie Faye turned back, looking triumphant even with her sunglasses on. "Everybody knows that."

Emma shook her head.

"But if that's what killed Alvin, then anyone in the county could be guilty," Hannah said.

"That many people have problems with clotting?" Dottie Faye kept her gaze trained on the man in the cowboy hat as he stood and got ready to leave. "Where do you suppose he goes?"

No one bothered to answer her.

"Every farm from here to Pennsylvania has rat poison," Hannah said.

"Hello, square one. Good to see you again." Kelly leaned back in her seat with a sigh.

"If only we could get our hands on the autopsy report," Emma mused.

Hannah shuddered.

"Sorry." Emma wrapped one arm around the woman and gave her a quick squeeze.

"Or the police report," Kelly added.

"He just left," Dottie Faye said. "I wonder ...." Without another word, she jumped up from the table and hurried to the front door.

"Alvin's funeral is today," Hannah said quietly.

"Oh, sweetie," Emma crooned, hugging her again. "I'm so sorry."

"Will you go with me?" She looked to Kelly. "Both of you?"

Attending a funeral was the last thing Emma wanted to do with her day, but maybe they would luck out and find more clues. Even better, maybe Hannah would remember the name of the student she had seen Rose with all those years ago. And Emma wanted to be there for her new friend.

"Of course we will," Kelly said, reaching across and taking Hannah's hand into her own.

A small smile trembled on Hannah's lips, but the moment was broken as Dottie Faye rushed back into the room. "You're not going to believe this. Cowboy Hat Man just drove away in a silver Mercedes!"

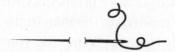

"Tell me again why we're doing this?" Emma tugged on the apron wrapped around her and wished this had happened in the fall. The weather was way too hot to go around in thick fabric and dark colors. At least posing as Mennonites, they got to wear a small print, even if it was black on navy. It was a good thing Dottie Faye had decided to stay at the B&B to keep a lookout for Cowboy Hat Man. She would have never passed for a Mennonite, disguise or not.

"Because you would never be allowed to attend the service otherwise." Hannah reached up and straightened the doily Kelly wore over her hair.

Together they walked into the barn.

A hush fell over the congregation as the three of them made their way between the two rows of benches to the front.

Emma tried to look like this wasn't her first Amish funeral. She kept her eyes ahead and tried not to stare at the casket as they slid onto the bench on the women's side of the barn.

Hannah's mother-in-law frowned at them as they settled in.

Emma wished they were sitting in the back. How else was she supposed to get a good look at those in attendance? There had to be three hundred people there, and the killer could easily have been among them.

She was about to say something to Hannah about it, but noticed the tears shimmering in her eyes. She took Hannah's hand into her own and squeezed it.

Alvin's mother frowned some more.

"I'm sorry," Hannah whispered. Emma wasn't sure who the words were directed at.

She squeezed her hand one more time, then let it go to keep the mother-in-law from having a coronary.

The bishop stood and cleared his throat. He spoke for about twenty minutes or so. Emma couldn't tell exactly, as she had had to leave all her jewelry, including her wristwatch, at the B&B.

Once the bishop finished speaking, a man she had never seen before rose and went to stand in front of the gathering. The congregation seemed to shift slightly as if settling in for a while. Emma glanced at Kelly, who, like her, was doing everything in her power not to turn around and scan the crowd. It certainly would have been a welcome distraction from the view of Alvin's body in the open casket.

After what seemed like an hour, Emma wanted to crawl to the back and sleep. Funerals were hard enough, but incredibly long funerals in a different language that she didn't speak were nothing short of torture. Still, she cast a reassuring smile to Hannah. She had come here to see if the killer would slip up and return to the scene of the crime, so to speak. But she had also come as Hannah's friend.

What did it say about Hannah's status in the Amish community that Emma and Kelly were her only friends?

Finally, the man uttered the magic word *Aemen*—even *she* could figure out what *that* meant—and the crowd of people stood. One by one, they filed in front of the casket, each gazing at Alvin Lapp for the last time. Mothers lifted the children too small to see the body from where they stood. There were a few tears, some head shaking, and sad looks shot toward Hannah. All in all, it was a quiet ceremony.

"Who are your friends, Hannah Lapp?" Alvin's mother asked once they, too, had walked in front of Alvin's casket.

Hannah cleared her throat. "These are my friends, Emma and Kelly."

"I don't remember seeing them around before." Her eyes narrowed as she sized them up. Did she recognize them from the mercantile?

"They're Mennonite," Hannah quickly explained. A little too quickly it seemed.

The older woman's eyes became mere slits.

"Emma, Kelly, this is Alvin's mother, Mary Lapp. Folks call her Daniel's Mary."

"*Goedemiddag,*" Emma carefully intoned, hoping the greeting didn't sound as forced as it felt. Hannah had taught Emma and Kelly both how to say "good afternoon," but that was all they'd had time to learn.

Thankfully, Daniel's Mary wasn't in a chatty mood, and she moved away without returning the words.

"OK," Kelly said.

"Is she always like that?" Emma asked.

"*Jah,*" Hannah answered. Emma felt for the poor woman. Daniel's Mary was the only relative Hannah had left except for distant cousins, and Mary acted like her daughter-in-law was something nasty stuck to the bottom of her shoe.

"We need to mill around," Emma said, nodding toward

the doors of the barn. Since the house was still considered a crime scene, the Lapp farm had been declared off-limits. Poor Hannah couldn't go home even if she wanted to.

Thank goodness for Casey. She'd lent them all clothes and hooked them up with the head coverings like the Mennonites wore.

"There'll be time for that," Hannah said. "Right now we need to go to the graveyard."

It was time to lay Alvin Lapp to rest.

Hannah drove them to the cemetery using the horse and buggy she had borrowed from Casey's brother. It was soothing, plodding along, the buggy swaying as the horse pulled them to their destination.

The buggy was a bit smaller than some of the others Emma had seen. Hannah told her that this was a courting buggy and not meant to hold a large Amish family. Regardless of size, they all had the same brown tops.

The cemetery was on the edge of town, right across from a much fancier one. Emma thought it a little odd that the two would be so close together despite their differences.

"That's the *Englisch* graveyard," Hannah said as they turned down the road lined with a simple wire fence.

All the graves were marked the same, with plain white tombstones. There was nothing more than names and dates of birth and death carved into the pale, cold rock. Even in death the Amish kept things plain.

Not everyone who had attended the service in the barn had come to the cemetery, but there were a good number of buggies in the slow procession.

Emma and Kelly gathered close to Hannah as she stood on one side of the grave, her glaring mother-in-law on the other. It was apparent that Daniel's Mary believed the sheriff had arrested the correct person. The bright rays of the sun could have been responsible for Mary's squint, but Emma was fairly certain there was more hatred involved than glare.

Somewhere near the road, a car door slammed, followed closely by another. But from where Emma was standing, she couldn't see the vehicle. Another followed. Or maybe she was hearing the echo from across the street. *Wishful thinking that the killer would show up here,* Emma thought.

The bishop stepped forward and said a few words, all of which were in Pennsylvania Dutch. Thankfully, it wasn't very long. Then Daniel's Mary and Hannah were invited to step forward and throw a handful of dirt onto the lowered casket. The pallbearers filled in the grave while the mourners watched. A few more words and another prayer, then the men replaced their hats, and everyone started back toward their buggies.

"Is that the man in the cowboy hat?" Emma asked, tugging on Kelly's sleeve.

"Not you too."

"I'm serious."

Kelly peered at the man as well. "I don't know. I've never seen him without his hat."

He had a build similar to the guest at the B&B. The man who accompanied him, however, was someone Emma had never seen before. They stood on the edge of the funeral crowd, glaringly out of place in their English clothes.

The two men turned to leave, and Emma lost sight of them. "Stay with Hannah," she instructed Kelly and took off through the crush.

She did her best to slow her pace to a brisk march when all she wanted to do was run. If the two men had come to the funeral in a silver Mercedes ....

Finally, she pushed through the crowd of people making

their way back to their buggies and saw the men get into a shiny red pickup. For a moment there she'd thought she was onto something.

"Well?" Kelly and Hannah joined her as the men pulled out into the street heading back through town.

Emma shook her head. "Red truck."

"Shoot," Kelly said.

"My sentiments exactly," Emma quipped.

"*Dunnerwetter*," Hannah said.

"Huh?" Emma and Kelly both turned toward her.

"We say '*dunnerwetter.*' At least not where the elders can hear us."

"What's that mean?" Kelly asked.

Hannah thought about it for a second. "Thunder weather."

"Oh, that's bad." Kelly tempered her words with a smile.

"So where do we go from here?" Emma asked.

Hannah sighed. "I'm expected back at my mother-in-law's *haus*. People will want to visit and tell stories about Alvin."

Emma inwardly cringed. Another afternoon spent being glared at by the good citizens of this community. That was just what she wanted to do. But one look at Hannah's face, and she knew she had to go.

"To Mary Daniels' house," Kelly said.

"Daniel's Mary," Hannah corrected.

"Why do they call her that?"

Hannah smiled. "I'll tell you in the buggy."

Emma and Kelly followed behind their newfound friend.

"Cheer up," Kelly told Emma. "There may be some *Englischers* at the wake."

Emma nodded. *And maybe one of them will be driving a shiny silver car.*

fifteen

Daniel's Mary looked none too happy about having Emma and Kelly in her home. Her name, it turned out, was a way to keep all the Mary Lapps from getting confused. She had married Daniel Lapp and became "Daniel's Mary." Word on the street was that it was not a name she was proud to have. In fact, the gossip from those days was that she wanted to be *the* Mary Lapp.

Emma and Kelly decided to stay quiet and out of the way. Emma figured that if she caused any trouble at all, Daniel's Mary would have the perfect excuse to ask them to leave. They took seats on hard chairs on either side of Hannah in this plain house that was much larger and brighter than Hannah and Alvin's.

All of the well-wishers offering condolences and ways to help almost brought tears to Emma's eyes. What a sight to see, neighbors helping neighbors. Despite all the problems and differences, they came through when it was needed most. When Emma said as much, Hannah shrugged. "It is just our way."

"Hannah Lapp." The booming voice reached them before the man did. He separated the crowd like Moses parting the Red Sea.

He came forward, his frown firmly in place. Emma couldn't help but notice that his pants were a couple of inches too short and showed a line of white where his shoes met his socks. He had the same chest-length beard as the surrounding men, but there was a hardness about him the others didn't possess. It was as if he were a little rougher around the edges than the rest.

"Deacon Beachy." Hannah nodded in greeting.

"This is for you." He handed her an envelope.

"*Danki.*" She ducked her head, but didn't open it.

"I wish there was more, but the community coffers are low right now."

"I understand." Hannah graced him with a small smile. "I appreciate any at all."

"The sheriff has not allowed you to return to your house yet?"

"*Nay,*" she said. "I am staying with friends." As she said the words, Daniel's Mary scowled.

"The church is here for you."

Hannah dipped her chin again. "*Danki,* Deacon."

"We have set up a collection box at the general store," he continued.

"Oh, *nay*. Please do not do that. I will only take away from little Joshua's fund."

"I appreciate your concern, but there is enough to go around." His words sounded confident, but the clouds in his eyes said something different. "My son is in the Lord's hands now."

"His will be done," Hannah murmured.

Deacon Beachy nodded and moved away.

"The little boy who fell out of the tree is the deacon's son?" Emma whispered.

"*Jah*. His only one. How do you know about this?"

"Dottie Faye saw the collection box," Emma explained.

"It's so sad," Kelly murmured.

"Why did he bring you money?" Emma asked.

"We have no insurance like the English. This is to help me get through without Alvin's income."

"Hannah, what are you going to do?" Emma asked.

She shrugged. "Continue to lease the land, I suppose. I do not have the skills to train the horses, but I can care for them."

Kelly sat up a little straighter in her seat. "That's it. The boy who helped Alvin with the horses. We need to talk to him. Maybe he saw something that day."

"Good idea," Emma agreed. Why hadn't they thought of that before?

Thirty minutes of sitting still, demurely smiling and pretending to be Mennonite, was about twenty-nine more than Emma could handle.

Finally, Emma spotted the lanky youngster with a shock of dark hair sticking out from underneath his plain straw hat. He was dressed identically to the men around him, but there was something about him, an energy that made him stand out even as he tried to blend in. It hadn't been so apparent when he was on the farm by himself, but here, surrounded by the members of his community, the differences shone like a beacon.

Kelly stood and rubbed her hands down the front of her dress. "I'll go talk to him."

Emma nodded. The poor boy might think they were ganging up on him if they both approached and starting asking questions.

"So, the money the deacon gave you, it comes from the same place as the money he's collecting for his son?"

Hannah nodded. "Not from the collection boxes, but from Amish Aid. We Amish take care of our own. Anytime sickness or tragedy strikes, the district collects money in a special fund to help those affected."

But what kind of money would it take to support a child with a broken neck? One confined to a wheelchair and declared paralyzed for life?

Kelly walked back over, her smile in direct opposition to Emma's sad thoughts.

"Good news," she said as she took her seat on the other side of Hannah.

"Yeah?" Emma said.

"Matthew did see something strange the day Alvin was murdered. He was on his way out after his chores when he saw a fancy silver car with two *Englischers* inside."

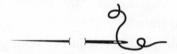

"At least we know we're on the right track." Kelly sighed.

"Now if we could get a break in solving Rose's murder," Emma said.

They were in the sitting area of their suite. Dottie Faye was out somewhere, and Hannah, overwhelmed by the events of the day, had gone into Emma's room to take a nap.

Being back in her own clothes felt wonderful to Emma, but she would do it all again in order to help Hannah.

"When Hannah gets up, let's show her the quilt blocks again," Kelly suggested.

Emma agreed. Not that she thought it would make a big difference. They had been showing Hannah the blocks and making her look at pictures on the school alumni page every spare moment they had with no luck. But it was better than doing nothing.

"Hello, chickadees." Dottie Faye burst into the suite, waving a stack of papers in front of her.

Emma and Kelly both shushed her.

"Hannah's trying to rest," Emma said.

"Oh." Dottie Faye lowered her voice and tiptoed into the room. "Rough day, huh?"

"You have no idea," Kelly said.

"Well, this should make it all better." She handed the papers to Emma.

Kelly scooted closer, reading over Emma's shoulder.

"The coroner's report on Alvin Lapp?" Emma looked back to her aunt. "How'd you get this?"

Dottie Faye shook her head. "A good reporter never reveals her sources."

"But you're not a reporter," Emma pointed out.

"Potato, potahto," she replied with a flick of her hand.

Emma shook her head and went back to the report.

"As you can see," Dottie Faye continued, "dearly departed Alvin was poisoned by none other than warfarin sodium. AKA, Coumadin. AKA, rat poison."

"And that narrows it down to everyone in the county," Emma said.

"Who said it had to end at the county line?" Kelly asked.

"Fine." Dottie Faye snatched the report back and stuffed it into her purse. "I can see you don't appreciate a good clue when you have it right in your hands."

Emma stood and wrapped her aunt in a quick hug. "You know we appreciate all you're doing to help."

Dottie Faye patted her hair back into place, but the fire had gone out of her eyes. "Sometimes I wouldn't know it."

The bedroom door opened, and Hannah stepped out into the living area. Her dress was wrinkled, and she had sleep creases on her face. But her prayer cap was straight and firmly pinned in place. "I heard shouting."

Dottie Faye moved across the room and threw one arm around Hannah's shoulders. "I'm sorry, sugar. I didn't know you were trying to sleep."

"I needed to get up anyway. All this laying around is making me lazy." She said the words, then flopped into the armchair.

Kelly smiled.

"I've got an idea," Dottie Faye said. "Let's retrace Alvin's steps from the week before he died. Maybe that will give us a place to start looking for rat poison. Though I have to admit, Ben the Baker is still at the top of my list."

Hannah frowned. "Did something happen?"

Emma told her about the autopsy report.

"So we know he was poisoned?" Hannah asked, her voice surprisingly calm. Maybe it was an Amish thing, to be able to let go of a loved one so easily and keep your emotions bottled up.

"It's all here in black and white." Dottie Faye patted her handbag.

"Do you remember what Alvin was doing the week before he died?" Emma asked.

Hannah bit her lip and shook her head.

"Anything out of the ordinary?" Kelly added.

"*Nay*," she said. "Well, there was one thing."

"Yes?" Excitement rose in Emma, but she tamped it back down. No use getting too worked up.

"He hired a Mennonite driver to take him someplace."

"Where?" Kelly asked, her gaze snagging Emma's.

"I do not know," Hannah said. "Alvin did not share the details of his business with me."

Emma wasn't surprised. Alvin was controlling to be sure, so why would he share something like his whereabouts with his wife?

Another dead end.

"But I know someone who might."

Emma perked up. "And who's that?"

"The driver."

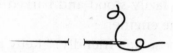

The Mennonite they were looking for lived a little way out of town and to the south. They were in Dottie Faye's Cadillac, Emma in the front seat with Dottie Faye, Kelly and Hannah in the back. Hannah slid down in her seat and covered her head with a towel so no one would see her in the car.

"Let me get this straight," Emma said as they drove. "You aren't allowed to even ride in a car?"

"Not unless it is an emergency," Hannah explained.

"Honey pie, I think this qualifies," Dottie Faye replied.

"That would be for the bishop and the elders to decide." Hannah raised the towel up and peeked around. Then she covered up again. "You want to take the next left."

"So, Alvin had an emergency?" Kelly asked.

"I really do not know."

"I know he didn't share much with you, but if he had an emergency, I'm sure he would have said something," Emma chimed in.

"Agreed," Kelly said.

Hannah pulled the towel from her head and straightened her little white cap. "I think we are far enough out that no one will recognize me." She said the words but remained slumped in her seat. "That is his house up there. I came here once with Alvin."

Dottie Faye turned the car down a short dirt lane that led to a pale blue, gingerbread-trimmed one-story. Flowers were planted all around, and a wooden swing sat in the shade of a large pin oak.

A yellow dog lazily stood and barked out a greeting as Dottie Faye cut the engine.

"Do you suppose he's friendly?" Kelly asked.

"Oh, *jah*," Hannah said.

As they got out of the car, a man opened the door of the house. He whistled for the dog as the screen door slammed behind him. He was dressed much the same as the Amish men in the community, though he wore a belt to keep his pants up and his shirt was a bright crimson. He had twinkling blue eyes and a stark white goatee.

"Hannah Lapp," he said, coming to greet her. He took her hands into his own. "I was so sorry to hear about Alvin."

Emma didn't remember seeing his face at the funeral that morning.

She noted that his accent was much the same as Hannah's as he continued. "I was planning to come out and see you, but I heard the sheriff still had your house roped off."

"*Jah*." She pulled away to introduce them to the Mennonite. "*Frenden*, this is John Petersheim."

They shook hands all around, and John invited them into the house. Once the niceties of lemonade and a plate of cookies were brought out, Emma got down to business. "We need to know where you took Alvin the day before he died," she said.

He leaned back in his chair and rubbed his thin goatee. It was such a contrast to the full beards Emma had grown used to seeing. "Well, I took him over to Herkimer, of course."

"Herkimer?" Hannah asked.

"Yes. That's where I always take him. Well, recently anyway."

"What's in Herkimer?" Emma asked.

"The horse stables," Hannah said.

John nodded his agreement.

"The man in the cowboy hat." Dottie Faye pounded one fist into her palm. "I knew it."

John frowned in confusion.

"Dottie Faye," Emma said gently.

Kelly let out a small sigh. "Just because horses are involved doesn't mean that cowboys are too."

"These are racehorses," John said.

"Thoroughbreds?" Emma asked, thinking about the horse she had seen Alvin with just days before he died.

John nodded.

"And you've taken him over there before?" she continued.

"Of course."

"Did you go with him around the stables? Did he meet anyone while he was there? Did you notice anything suspicious?" The questions tumbled out of Emma's mouth one on top of the other.

John shook his head. "This was his business. I dropped him off at the stable office, then drove to the closest restaurant to have a cup of coffee while I waited."

"Did you see a silver Mercedes?" Dottie Faye asked. "Or a tall man in a cowboy hat?"

"Or anything out of the ordinary?" Emma added.

"No." He stopped, seeming to think for a minute before he continued. "Well, there was one thing."

"Yes." Emma leaned forward in her chair to catch every word he said.

"Alvin was in a fine mood on the way there. Cheerful even."

"Alvin?" Hannah asked. "My Alvin?"

John nodded. "But when I went to pick him up, he was angry. Really angry."

"That is more like him," Hannah said.

"I got the feeling he'd been arguing with whoever it was he went to meet."

sixteen

"**Y**ou know where we have to go now," Kelly said as they got back into the car. They had thanked John Petersheim, and he'd made Hannah promise to bring him one of her famous cherry pies.

Evidently, word of the poisoning hadn't made it to the Mennonites yet. Or maybe the sheriff was keeping that a secret for his own gain.

Dottie Faye pulled a GPS from the glove box, to Emma's chagrin, and punched Herkimer, New York, into it.

"I thought you got rid of the GPS," Emma said. "Something about it being too bossy."

"Well, I changed my mind. This Yankee-voiced contraption stays in the dark most of the time. Besides, sometimes a girl's gotta do what a girl's gotta do."

Half an hour later, they pulled into the parking lot of a flat-roofed building made of natural stone. Beautiful stained-wood horse stables stretched out behind the building, and white board fences zigzagged across the lush green pastures.

"Would you look at this place?" Dottie Faye got out of the car and turned in a full circle to take it all in.

Hannah got out of the car, glancing around as if the devil himself were about to jump out and cart her away. She seemed tiny and terribly out of place.

"I thought it would be busier than this." Emma gestured to the nearly empty parking lot. There were a couple of cars, but none of them was a silver Mercedes.

She had to admit the place was beautiful. A wood-and-stone sign with yellow flowers planted all around declared the place to be Stanley Stables.

"I wonder if they named this place after the Stanley Cup," Dottie Faye mused.

Kelly rolled her eyes, but couldn't hide her smile.

"That's hockey, Dottie Faye," Emma said.

Her aunt shrugged.

"Hey, that's the truck from the funeral." Emma pointed toward a dusty red truck parked to one side of the office. "Well, it looks like it might be. I mean, they're both red."

"What are the odds?" Kelly asked.

Dottie Faye pulled her cellphone from her purse and started punching in numbers.

"Let's go." Emma marched to the door and pulled it open.

Inside, a man sat behind a huge desk made of gleaming cherry wood in a deep emerald-green office with framed pictures of jockeys on horses with ribbons attached. An antique-looking saddle perched on a fancy sawhorse, a memory of horse racing days past.

He looked up as they entered, his eyes narrowing as he caught sight of Hannah. "Can I help you ladies?"

"We understand that you have business dealings with Alvin Lapp from Fort Plain." Emma had decided that upfront and confident was the way to go. She only wished she felt as poised as she sounded.

"I do." His chair squeaked as he leaned back and laced his fingers behind his head.

"Did you know this was the last place he visited before he was murdered?" Emma asked.

"Are you ladies with the police?" He looked at them, from one to another, as if testing to see if they'd tell him the truth.

"Because if you are, I'm going to need to see some badges."

Hannah stepped forward. "I am Alvin's widow, Hannah Lapp." She extended a hand for him to shake.

"It's a pleasure." He stood and took her hand into his for a quick pump, then released it. "David Wilson."

"I wanted to come tell you that I will not be able to train the horses like Alvin did, but you are welcome to lease the land for your beasts," Hannah said.

Emma was afraid the man might burst out laughing. There was enough land here to build a town. So why did he need Alvin Lapp and his twenty-acre farm?

"Oh. Alvin wasn't training the horses, he was rehabbing them."

Hannah tilted her head to one side as if trying to figure out exactly what the man was telling her.

"You know," Kelly added. "Helping them get better after they'd been hurt."

The man smiled, seemingly pleased that one of them understood his meaning.

"Why can't you care for them here?" Emma asked, regretting that the question burst from her. There was plenty of land, plenty of room in the stables, and surely enough staff on hand to spoon-feed a horse if need be.

The man's smile turned plastic. "If that's all, ladies, I have work to return to."

"Do you mind if we take a look around?" Emma asked.

He shook his head. "I'm sorry, tours have to be scheduled at least a week in advance in order for me to have the staff on hand to take care of it."

"What about rats?" Kelly asked. She crossed her arms as if settling in until she got some answers.

"I beg your pardon?" Once again he sat back as if

trying to decide if he should answer their question or kick them out.

"It must be mur ... a *chore* to keep rats under control with all the space you have here," Kelly continued.

He shook his head gently, but his eyes had turned cold. "We do what we can."

"Poison?" she pressed.

"Never." The one word was clipped. "We stuff holes and cracks with steel wool. That keeps most vermin out, and we've planted mint all around the buildings. It may be an old wives' tale, but you can't be too careful."

"No poison?" Kelly persisted.

His eyes and his voice turned into a matched set of steel. "Someone might get hurt."

"Or the horses," Kelly added.

"That's exactly what I mean," he said.

"One hundred thousand to one!" Dottie Faye shouted triumphantly. She looked around at all the serious faces. "The odds of the truck ... oh, never mind." She put her phone back in her purse.

The man behind the desk gave them a dismissive nod. "Now if you'll excuse me."

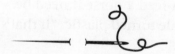

The ride back to the B&B was a quiet one. Emma wondered if Hannah was thinking about what she would finally do when the stable came to get the horses on her property. How would she care for herself?

Tea was long since over, and it was still too early to head to the diner.

"Look." Dottie Faye pointed to the counter. A collection box for Joshua Beachy sat off to one side. "That is a shame," she tsked. "So young and never gonna walk again. Just a shame."

"Looks like Sylvia's been busy." A large cardboard box like the one Ben the Baker used sat behind the check-in desk.

"I didn't realize they would go through so many pies here," Kelly said.

"They're full right now. I heard Casey say something to the cook," Hannah added.

"And they have that big Cowboy Hat Man eating. I'm sure he can put away a pie or two," Dottie Faye said.

Emma shook her head, and the four of them trudged up the stairs, their thoughts as heavy as their footfalls.

"Maybe I'll take a look at the quilt blocks again," Hannah said as Dottie Faye dug out the key and inserted it into the lock.

"That'd be fine," Emma murmured. Why was Hannah trying to make her feel better when her own future hung in the balance?

Dottie Faye pushed open the door.

"What the heck?"

The common area was a mess. No, those words were too kind for the sight that greeted them. It was a wreck. Cushions had been torn from the couch and scattered across the room. The coffee table was overturned, the vase containing flowers strewn aside and dripping water onto the floor.

"Oh, my," Hannah gasped.

Emma's breath caught in her throat.

"Do you think he followed us here?" Kelly asked, referring to their stalker.

It was the question on all of their minds. Had *he* been driving that silver car? Had *he* destroyed their suite?

Emma dropped her purse onto the back of the armchair and rushed into the bedroom. Her room was in the same shape as the living area. Clothes strewn about, her suitcases open and lying empty on the floor. The bed was stripped, the covers thrown to the floor. She knelt down next to the overturned nightstand and pushed her hands between the mattress and box springs. She let out a sigh of relief when she encountered the quilt blocks. She had put them there for safekeeping, and she was so thankful that she had.

"Emma." Dottie Faye was right behind her. In her hand she carried a bottle of Chanel No. 5 in the 'ready to spray' position. "Don't go running off like that. What if he's still here?"

Emma pushed to her feet. "He's not still here."

"You don't know that," Kelly said from the doorway. "Hannah." She turned back toward the living area. "Don't touch anything. We have to call the police."

Dottie Faye nodded. "She's right."

Emma recalled the sheriff and his good ol' boy attitude. He was the last person she wanted to call. But this had to be reported.

She picked her way out of the room and back to where she left her purse. "Here." She handed her phone to Kelly. "You call. I think he likes you better anyway."

Kelly took the phone but didn't comment.

"And the front desk too."

Kelly looked around. "I suppose it would be too much to ask that someone in the B&B saw who did this."

"Dottie Faye, would you stop that?" Her aunt was creeping around the room, perfume bottle upright and ready as she peeked behind doors and into the coat closet. "Whoever did this is long gone by now."

"Can't be too sure about that," she said cryptically.

Emma shook her head and perched on the sofa's armrest. "There are no windows open and no balconies on this floor. So whoever came in here," she said, pointing to the main door to the room, "came through there."

"What if there are secret passages, huh?" Dottie Faye raised her expressive brows.

"Maybe." Emma sighed. This trip was turning into so much more than she'd bargained for.

"You never know with houses like this."

"The sheriff's on his way." Kelly tapped the screen and handed the phone back to Emma.

"We should probably get some pictures of this." She gestured toward the destroyed room.

"Wouldn't the sheriff do that?" Dottie Faye asked.

Kelly shot her a look.

"Yeah, right," she said, each word one more syllable longer than even her Southern drawl demanded.

"My room's the same," Kelly said, disappearing inside.

"I'm so sorry," Hannah cried. She wrapped her arms around her middle, sobs shaking her entire body.

"There, there," Dottie Faye soothed, finally abandoning her guardianship by fragrance and tucking Hannah into her side. Three seconds flat and she was in full-on mothering mode. "It's going to be all right."

"But none of this would have happened if you had not been helping me."

"Oh, hush that," she chided. "Take a picture of the couch, Emma. We're sitting down in less than a heartbeat."

Emma snapped off a couple of pictures on her phone and replaced the cushions. Surely the sheriff couldn't find fault in that.

"Emma," Kelly called from the bathroom doorway. "You'd better come see this."

The bathroom was in much the same state as the rest of the suite, with toiletries and towels scattered about. But most chilling of all was the message written in red on the mirror above the sink: "English go home."

"Ever get the feeling someone doesn't want us here?" Emma asked.

"Only on days that end in *y*."

Dottie Faye appeared behind them and gasped. "My lipstick!" She moved to snatch the tube from the counter.

"No!" Emma and Kelly shouted at the same time. "It might have fingerprints on it."

Dottie Faye pouted. "But it is brand new. I haven't even worn it yet."

"Didn't you put it on last night after supper?" Kelly asked.

"I've only worn it once," Dottie Faye amended.

"Gut himmel!"

Emma squeezed around Dottie Faye to exit the bathroom. Casey stood on the other side of the threshold, one foot lifted as if she were about to step inside, then thought better of it.

"Casey," Emma greeted her. "The sheriff is on his way."

She nodded and finally placed her foot back onto the floor. "I was in the other suite, and I thought I heard a scream."

"It's something, huh?" Kelly quipped.

Emma knew her friend well enough to understand that a little bit of humor could cover up a great deal of anxiety.

"I think I should go tell Sylvia what has happened." Casey took a half-step back.

"Because she evidently didn't believe me," Kelly mumbled under her breath.

Casey turned on her heel and ran smack into the sheriff.

Ol' Roy Johnson himself had come out for this one. Sylvia Yoder was right behind him.

"Excuse me," Casey muttered and rushed out of sight.

The sheriff tipped his hat back and stepped into the room. "Well now, what have we here?"

"We took a car trip today, and when we came back, this is what we found," Emma explained.

Sylvia stepped in as well. Picking her way through the strewn items, was obviously taking her own mental inventory of the damage.

"Anything missing?" the sheriff asked.

"Not that we can tell," Emma said. "But we didn't want to touch anything in case the vandal left fingerprints on anything."

He gave a regal nod. "Any idea who did it?"

It was on the tip of Emma's tongue to tell him that if she had any idea, she wouldn't have bothered to call him to investigate.

Sylvia twisted her fingers in her pearls before sadly shaking her head. "Never in my twenty years as an innkeeper has anything like this ever happened."

"That's not even the worst part," Dottie Faye whined. "They destroyed my new lipstick." She pointed to the bathroom, where the tragedy had occurred.

Sheriff Roy stepped into the room and nodded once to Hannah, who had managed to pull herself together. "Mrs. Yoder, you can go back downstairs for now. I've got this."

She hesitated, then nodded, still clutching her pearls.

"Just don't go anywhere," he added. "We'll need a statement later."

The tension level in the room dropped slightly as Sylvia Yoder left to attend her regular duties.

"It was a fifteen-dollar tube," Dottie Faye continued as the sheriff took a mental image of the bathroom.

"Fifteen dollars? For drugstore lipstick?" Emma wanted to slap her hand over her mouth, but it was too late. The words were out.

"It's a good brand." Dottie Faye propped her hands on her hips. "And a hard-to-find color."

Emma knew better than to engage Dottie Faye over something as earth-shattering as lipstick.

"What do you make of it?" Kelly asked Sheriff Roy.

"Well, Kelly Grace, it looks as though you have angered someone here in Fort Plain."

You think?

"And?" Kelly prompted. "Aren't you going to take pictures or write a report or something?"

The sheriff took a handkerchief from his back pocket and wiped his forehead around where his hat usually rested.

"My deputy will be here shortly to do all of that. In the meantime, you should go downstairs and not worry your pretty little heads about it. We'll be busy in here for a while." He looked around the room once again. His gaze was lazy, but Emma had a feeling there was more intelligence beneath his façade than he was letting on. "Why did you say you came here again?" he asked.

"To visit our friend Hannah Lapp." The lie slid easily from her lips. Maybe too easily. She still didn't trust the sheriff, not even as far as she could throw him.

"One thing's certain. You've touched a nerve with somebody," he said. He turned his hard eyes to each of them in turn. "If I were you, I'd lay low for a little while. Stop asking questions and stirring up dust. You've ruffled somebody's feathers. Think hard before you poke a stick at a hornet's nest."

seventeen

The sheriff wouldn't let them touch anything until his deputy had taken their statements and ran a check for fingerprints. The four headed down to the diner, knowing the police work would take the better part of the evening.

"I don't know about you girls, but I could use some pie," Dottie Faye said as they slid into their favorite booth.

"Ditto." Kelly pushed her menu aside.

"What does this mean, 'ditto'?" Hannah asked.

"It means that you agree with what the other person said," Emma explained.

Hannah nodded. "Oh," she said slowly.

Emma had the feeling she was no clearer on the meaning after the explanation than she had been before.

Hannah propped her elbow on the table and rested her chin in her hand. "I am going to miss you when you have to leave." She smiled, but her eyes shone with a thin mist of tears.

"That's sweet of you to say, sugar." Dottie Faye patted her shoulder.

"I am being truthful. I am sorry that Alvin is dead, but being with the three of you has added something more to my life. I am grateful, well and truly."

No more was said as the waitress stopped at their table to take their orders. They requested cherry pie all around and decaf coffee.

"Uh-oh." Kelly nodded toward the front of the diner. Staring through the large plate-glass window was Daniel's Mary.

Hannah swiveled in her seat, saw her mother-in-law, then faced the front, turning away from the cold, staring eyes.

The woman continued to stare as Emma asked, "Is she going to make your life hard from now on?" Daniel's Mary certainly didn't seem to be handling her grief very well. Or maybe it was her hatred that was at work.

"Perhaps when she does not believe that I killed Alvin, she will be kinder to me." The tone of Hannah's voice didn't hold much hope.

"Maybe," Emma said. Out of the corner of her eye she saw Daniel's Mary move away from the window and continue down the sidewalk. If she hadn't figured out by now that they weren't Mennonite, it was a miracle. She hoped that didn't add to Hannah's troubles.

The waitress arrived with their pie, and the conversation stilled as they began to eat.

An idea niggled in the back of Emma's mind, something she couldn't quite put her finger on.

"Do you get the feeling we've missed something?" she asked the others. "Something big? Important, even."

Dottie Faye licked the tangy pie filling off of her fork with an expression of sheer ecstasy. "I can't think of much else with something this delicious sitting in front of me."

"Ditto," Hannah said.

The four of them laughed. Maybe Hannah understood after all.

"What I want to know is who would want to ruin my lipstick that way." Dottie Faye took a sip of her coffee, her blue eyes as serious as Emma had ever seen them.

"It could have been anybody." Emma thought it best to ignore the lipstick comment.

Kelly nodded. "But we know that Ben Lambright was at the B&B while we were gone. He brought in pies."

"Or someone from his shop did," Emma pointed out.

"And the deacon," Dottie Faye answered. "There was a collection box for his son."

"Why would the deacon not want us here?" Kelly asked.

"Maybe because you bring to his mind my sins with the church," Hannah mused.

"Could be." But Emma wasn't convinced.

"It could not be him," Hannah said, echoing Emma's doubts. "We are a peaceful people. He would never do such a thing."

Emma didn't bother to point out that murder had just been committed in a 'peaceful' community.

"I'm serious though," Emma continued. She couldn't rid herself of that feeling, that left-the-stove-on or the-door's-unlocked sinking in her stomach.

"Maybe you just need a good night's rest," Kelly suggested.

Emma shrugged.

"Or another piece of this pie." Dottie Faye scraped the last bite from her plate and popped it into her mouth.

"*Ach*, it is *gut*," Hannah agreed. "The crust is so flaky."

A light went off somewhere in Emma's brain. "The crust!" she exclaimed, pointing to her half-eaten slice. There on the outer edge was the braiding used only by Ben Lambright.

"Would you look at that," Dottie Faye murmured.

Kelly's eyes lit up. "And that means—"

"That whoever poisoned Alvin's pie may not have bought it from the bakery." Emma waved to the waitress.

She hurried over, coffeepot in hand. "Is everything all right over here?"

"Delicious," Dottie Faye said, though her mind didn't seem to be on pie any longer.

"Tell me," Emma said. "I thought that Ben Lambright was the only one in the county that used this braiding on his pie crusts."

The waitress, Cris according her name badge, nodded. "That's right."

"But this pie has that detail." Emma gestured toward her plate.

"That's because it's a Lambright pie."

Kelly frowned. "I don't understand."

Cris propped one hand on her hip. "Sometimes we don't have time to bake all the pies we need." She dropped her voice. "The cook doesn't like to make cherry pie. Your guess is as good as mine as to why. Ask for a coconut cream, and all is right with the world. Ask for a cherry, and run for the hills."

"So, you don't make the cherry pies here. You get them from the bakery."

"Yes, ma'am."

"Does anyone ever buy a whole pie?" Kelly asked.

"Oh, sure. Lots of times."

Emma snagged Kelly's gaze. Was this the break they'd been looking for? "On Monday did you sell a pie to a man who doesn't live here? He may have been driving a silver Mercedes." Her question sounded weak at best, but it was all she had to go on.

Cris shook her head, her ponytail swishing behind her. "I don't work on Mondays. I take a class over at the tech school. But Melinda was here."

Yes! "Is Melinda here now?"

She checked her watch. "Her shift starts in fifteen. She should be here soon."

"Thanks," Emma said. Fifteen minutes wasn't too long to wait for what might be the break they'd been looking for.

Emma made a mental note to leave Cris a great big tip.

Ten minutes later, a tall brunette bounced into the diner. She wore the same style T-shirt as Cris.

"That must be Melinda," Dottie Faye said under her breath.

"I hope so," Emma replied. Fifteen minutes wasn't typically a long time to wait, but it was when a person was anxious and had nothing to do but eat, check the time, and breathe.

Melinda tied an apron around her middle as Cris talked to her behind the counter. She must have been telling Melinda about the questions they had asked her. Melinda looked over to where they sat and gave a quick nod.

It seemed like an eternity before she moved from behind the counter and came to stand at their table. "Cris said you wanted to ask me something."

"On Monday, did a man come in here and buy a whole cherry pie?"

Melinda tapped her chin thoughtfully. "Monday," she repeated. "Monday, Monday. You know, I think so."

Emma's heart pounded. "Do you remember what he looked like?"

"He was a big guy, brawny, you know. Kinda tall. About sixty, I would say."

"Did he wear a cowboy hat?" Dottie Faye asked.

"Dottie Faye!" Emma exclaimed.

Melinda shook her head. "No cowboy hat, but he was balding and had one of those comb-over dos. I remember because he wasn't from around here, and he didn't look like the touristy type."

If only she had gotten a closer look at the guys at the funeral.

"Did you happen to see what he was driving?"

"That was the other thing," Melinda said. "He was driving a red truck." She shook her head. "Well, he was the passenger.

I wouldn't have noticed, but the driver started honking at him. I guess he was taking too long."

Emma smiled and looked around at her companions. They returned her grin all around.

"Does that help you any?"

"Sugar," Dottie Faye said, tucking a fifty-dollar bill into Melinda's hand, "that helps us a lot."

"Are we going back to the stables now?" Hannah asked as they stepped out into the waning daylight.

As much as Emma wanted to jump in the car and head straight to Herkimer and the Stanley Stables, she knew it would have to wait. She shook her head. "It'll be dark soon. Who knows if anybody is there this time of day."

"As much as I hate to admit it, I think you're right," Kelly said.

"Maybe you should call the sheriff," Dottie Faye suggested, then started to laugh.

"Why is that funny?" Hannah asked.

"I don't think the sheriff likes us very much," Emma explained.

"That's an understatement," Dottie Faye added.

"Herkimer is in a different county. Perhaps the sheriff there would be more willing to help," Hannah offered.

"Or not." Kelly shook her head. "I say we get up in the morning and head over that way. Maybe we can catch someone by surprise."

"Or we could really luck out," Emma added, "and there'll be no one there at all."

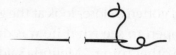

The morning dawned sunny and beautiful, but by the time they had dressed and eaten breakfast, the sky had turned an ugly shade of gray.

"Looks like a storm's coming," Sylvia said as she gazed out the common room windows.

Emma hoped it wasn't a dark omen about their day.

"Are you ready?" Kelly glanced at each of them in turn.

Hannah nodded. The sheriff had released her house the night before. He'd called the B&B to let her know. Emma had driven her out to pick up some clean clothes, but she didn't have the heart to make her stay in the dark house by herself. They'd gathered up her things and headed back into town.

Dottie Faye pinched the bridge of her nose and squinted. "Y'all go on without me. I feel a migraine coming on."

"All that running around and excitement yesterday," Kelly said.

"Or maybe you just want to keep tabs on Cowboy Hat Man," Emma joked.

Dottie Faye shook her head. "I think it's the rain."

Emma nodded. "We'll be back as soon as we can. I have my cellphone if you need me."

"Be careful." Dottie Faye handed her the keys to the Cadillac and kissed her cheek. Emma felt the slick smear of her lipstick, but she waited until her aunt was climbing the stairs before taking a napkin and wiping at the stain. "Is it all gone?"

Kelly studied her. "You got it."

"Let's go then."

They filed out of the B&B and climbed into the car. They had been to Herkimer one time, but Emma wasn't taking any chances. She punched their destination into the GPS, and they were off.

"What are we going to do when we get there?" Hannah asked from the backseat.

Emma shrugged. "Let's play it by ear. You go in and start talking business with the man. Land leases, that sort of thing. You think you can do that?"

Hannah nodded. "But I don't know much about business."

"It's OK," Kelly added. "What you don't know you can make up."

"Tell him you have a cousin who is coming to stay with you. He's an excellent horse trainer, and you want to keep Alvin's contracts with the stables."

A frown creased Hannah's brow. "But that is not the truth."

"You've got to tell him something. I'm sure you'll be forgiven for telling one little white lie in order to bring your husband's killer to justice."

Hannah pressed her lips together, then gave a small nod. "I suppose you are right about that."

"Kelly, you get your phone ready. Record everything that's said. With any luck we can get him to talk to us a little more. Maybe we can get him to admit to attending the funeral or even visiting Alvin the day he died."

"Then we can potentially place him at the scene of the crime, silver car or no silver car."

"I do not know if I have said this before," Hannah started, "and I surely cannot say it enough. *Danki* for helping me. I do not know what I would have done without you."

"Something would have come up," Kelly said with confidence.

Hannah shook her head. "I am well and truly blessed."

Emma was saved having to answer as her phone rang.

Kelly fished it out of her purse and tapped the screen before handing it to Emma.

"Hello?"

"Hello, sweet pea." Dottie Faye. "Would you be a dear and on your way home pick me up some Tylenol?"

Emma cast a quick glance at Kelly. "Of course." *She wants Tylenol,* Emma mouthed.

Kelly nodded.

"Thanks, sugar. I'm going to take a nap until you get back."

"Just rest." They said their goodbyes, then Emma thumbed the phone off and tossed it into the console.

"She's still got a headache?" Kelly asked.

Emma nodded. "It's so unlike her."

The first of the raindrops started to fall as they pulled into the stables. A couple of stock trucks were parked off to one side. There was no sign of the red truck or a silver car.

"What do we do now?" Hannah asked as Emma parked.

"I don't know," Emma answered. "Let me think on it a minute."

"I guess we could wait until they get here. Maybe it's too early for them," Kelly said.

"I bet somebody's here. A stable hand or something," Emma replied.

The rain started beating down on the roof of the car.

"You really want to get out and try to figure out a way into the stables in this mess?" Kelly asked.

Emma shook her head and peered out the window toward the lowering sky. "Not particularly, no."

"We could wait it out," Hannah said. "Maybe by then someone will come in for us to talk to."

Emma looked at Kelly who was staring right back. "Are you thinking what I'm thinking?"

"If you're thinking we should see if the door's unlocked, then I am."

"You are just going to walk in?" Hannah asked.

Kelly nodded. "Yep."

Hannah's eyes grew wide with fear. Apparently her adventuresome spirit still needed a little work. "I think I'll stay here if you do not mind."

Emma shrugged. "Suit yourself."

"Ready?" Kelly asked.

Emma nodded. "Ready."

The best was to make a run for it. They hopped out of the car and sprinted toward the building. Despite their hustle, they were both soaked by the time they reached the small alcove-type porch.

"You know if God loves us, that door will be unlocked," Kelly said with a smile.

"Don't say that," Emma admonished, but when she tried the door, it opened without protest.

"Whaddya know?" Kelly said, her grin widening.

The front office looked the same as it had the previous day except that David Wilson, His Royal Rudeness, was nowhere in sight.

Emma wiped her hands on her jeans. "You look in the filing cabinet, and I'll search the desk."

"Check." Kelly moved toward the three standing filing cabinets. "Not sure what I'm looking for," she said. "Any files labeled 'Illegal Activities' or 'How I Killed Alvin Lapp'?"

"Anything that looks suspicious." Emma tried the top drawer. It opened smoothly but contained nothing more incriminating than a stapler.

Kelly was going down the row of drawers, pulling on each one with no success.

Emma tugged on the big bottom drawer of the desk only to find it locked as well.

"Emma." Kelly's voice crackled with excitement. "I think I found something."

"Really?" She whirled around to face her friend.

Kelly held an opened ledger in her trembling hands. "This is a medication schedule. They've been injecting horses with some sort of painkiller."

Emma thought about it for a second, an article she had recently read in the local paper coming to mind. "That would make them run faster, because they couldn't feel pain during the race."

"Then they bet on the long shot and win. It's all right here," Kelly said.

"But that's—"

"Illegal," said a male voice from the doorway.

eighteen

"**W**hy don't you move right on over there next to your friend?" David Wilson motioned for Kelly to go stand next to Emma.

At least he didn't have a gun. *Lord, please don't let him have a gun.*

"I'll take that." He plucked the ledger from Kelly's fingers.

"So, you killed Alvin Lapp." Kelly moved a little closer to Emma.

Emma shot Kelly a "Will you be quiet?!" look, but Kelly nodded her head as if to say, *I got this.* Emma certainly hoped so.

"No." He shook his head. "Not me."

"But you know who did," Kelly said. "You were a part of it."

"No," he said again. "I'm only in it for the horses."

"What about the horses?" Kelly persisted.

Emma realized she was trying to distract him.

"I didn't want Alvin to die," the man said. "But he found out what we were doing and was going to go to the authorities with it."

His use of the word *we* was not lost on Emma. There was a partner still out there somewhere.

Kelly moved a little closer, dropping back a step so that her shoulder was behind Emma's.

"So instead of cutting him in, you cut him out, so to speak." Emma released a stifled laugh at her own poor attempt at a joke. She had to keep him talking while Kelly tried to inconspicuously dig her cellphone from her purse. Distraction was the only hope they had. She had left her phone in the car with Hannah, who likely didn't even know what a cellphone was.

Smart move, Cotton.

"You don't understand." He began to pace. "There are millions of dollars at stake."

He stopped and stared at them as if just now realizing they were there. Then he stalked toward them, his hand out. "Give it here." He wiggled his fingers encouragingly. "The phone," he continued. "Now."

Kelly sighed and handed him their last hope for getting away. Unless ....

If he had a gun, surely he would have pulled it out by now. He had Alvin poisoned; it wasn't like he was trigger-happy. If his partner was really the one who had killed Alvin, all the better. Maybe with a little teamwork, she and Kelly could take him.

Was it worth the risk?

"It wasn't supposed to be like this." He shoved Kelly's phone into his pocket and tossed the ledger onto a nearby chair. Once his hands were free, he ran his fingers through his hair. It stood on end like the quills of a porcupine.

"What did you expect, really?" Kelly asked.

Emma elbowed her. Sure, they needed to keep the man talking. She just wasn't sure this was the best topic.

"No one was supposed to get hurt."

"What are you going to do with us?" Kelly asked.

"You can't poison us," Emma added.

"And you don't have a gun."

Lord, please, please don't let him have a gun.

"You can't keep us here forever," Kelly continued.

"It's over," Emma said quietly.

"I'm not going to jail for this," he stated. "This wasn't even my idea."

"Whose idea was it?" Kelly asked. "The man in the cowboy hat?" They started to inch around toward the door. If they took small enough steps, perhaps he wouldn't notice until it was too late.

"What?" He stopped once again, pinning them with a wild stare.

"Never mind," Kelly said.

They inched a little closer to the door.

"Not even the horses were to be harmed," he said. "This stuff ... he told me that it was all natural, from some frog in the Brazilian rain forest."

Emma looked to Kelly. *Frog?* She mouthed.

Kelly shrugged.

"It's not even a drug, really. But I don't think the racing commissioner will overlook that."

"Let us go," Emma said. "You don't want to add kidnapping to your list of crimes."

Well, it wasn't exactly kidnapping, but she couldn't think of the right word under such pressure.

"What to do? What to do?" He paced in small steps, never taking his eyes from them. "I've gotta think."

"You should just let us go," Emma said. "If you didn't kill Alvin Lapp, then what are you doing holding us?"

"Seems to me that you're practically innocent," Kelly added.

"I would not go as far as to say that."

Emma turned to see a man in the shadowy alcove. He took a step forward, surveying the scene before him with barely veiled contempt.

Deacon Beachy. Emma recognized him from the funeral.

He was the man who had brought Hannah money to tide her over after Alvin's death.

She didn't waste a minute wondering why he was there. They were saved!

"Deacon! Thank goodness you're here." Emma took a step toward him, but stopped when he pinned her with a cold stare and the barrel of a gun.

An Amish man with a gun!

"Why do you *Englischers* keep turning up all over my district?"

"I, uh-um, didn't think your district extended all the way to Herkimer," Kelly said.

Emma took a step back, standing shoulder to shoulder with Kelly once again.

"It does if I say it does."

So, not saved.

The man from the stables turned to the deacon. "What are we going to do with them? I don't want anyone else to get hurt."

"Well, that seems unfortunate for all of you. Surely you understand that, like Alvin, they know our little secret and therefore have to be dealt with."

"Us?" Emma laughed, a choked sound. "We don't know anything."

"You know enough." His dark tone sent chills down her spine.

"Why are you doing this?" Emma asked.

Once again, the deacon lifted his gaze to hers. "Money."

"I thought the Amish weren't into such things," Kelly said. "What happened to the simple life and having only what you need?"

The deacon laughed, but the sound was bitter. "That is

all well and good until you have a paralyzed child. Do you have any idea how much treatment costs? Of course you do not. You have your insurance and fancy ways. I had to help my boy. This was the only way."

"But we saw the collection boxes," Emma said. Maybe if she kept him talking, they would stall him long enough that someone would come in, a stable hand or a trainer. He wouldn't kill all of them, would he?

The cold light in his eyes said he was past the point of desperation. "The people mean well, but those boxes only bring in a pittance. I will not let my son suffer any more than he already has." He swung his attention to the trainer. "David, tie them up."

"With what?" he asked.

"This is a horse stable. Surely there is a length of rope around somewhere."

David glanced about the room as if he would find it among the bookshelves and filing cabinets.

"David," Kelly said, "you don't think he's going to let you live too?"

"Be quiet," the deacon barked.

David's gaze continued his search, but Emma knew he was thinking about what Kelly had said.

"If he killed Alvin Lapp, why would he let you get off scot-free?" Emma added.

"I said be quiet!"

"I'll have to go to the barn and get some rope," David said.

Emma couldn't tell if he was being truthful or if he was looking for a way out.

"For pity's sake." The deacon gritted his teeth.

The man was under a great deal of stress, and Emma was afraid that any minute he might snap. His face above his beard was as red as a beet. His free hand was clenched into a fist, but the one holding the pistol was steady. His eyes flashed with a desperation she could only imagine.

"Take off your belt," the deacon said.

"Huh?" Apparently David was as clueless as Emma.

"Take off your belt and use it to tie them up."

Kelly tossed her head. "That'll never work. There are two of us and one little piece of leather."

Of course the piece of leather in question looked as thick as a python and twice as strong.

"It was a perfect plan," the deacon said as David took off his belt. He turned it this way and that as if trying to decide the best way to use it to bind two people. "I had the stuff flown in from South America. Once it hit the Amish community, it went completely off the radar."

"Of course," Emma said. "Who would expect an Amish deacon to be involved in fixing horse races?"

"Exactly."

"David," Emma whispered as he approached, belt in hand, "you don't have to do this."

He shook his head. "I'm in too deep."

"There's still a way out," Kelly added. "But if you help him and kill us, then there won't be."

"How many people have to die?" Emma asked.

"It's not that simple. We've had it tough the past couple of years. This was my way out of the hole." Sweat beaded on his forehead despite the comfortable temperature in the room. They were getting to him.

"If you end up in prison, won't that be worse?" Kelly asked.

"We're not going to prison," David said, but his voice cracked on the last word. Gone was the confident man who had kicked them out of his office, and in his place was a trembling mess of nerves. "I can't go to prison. I've got kids."

His voice rose just enough for the deacon to hear. "We've all got kids, David. And we have to do what we must to take care of them."

"I ...."

She could feel him faltering.

"I don't know how to tie them with this thing." He wiped the sweat from his face.

"Turn them back-to-back and lash their hands together."

David jostled them around until she and Kelly had their hands secured behind them. He had made his decision to join the dark side. Now their only hope was Hannah. Emma closed her eyes and willed Hannah to call the police. It was a dumb thing to do, but it was all she had left.

If Hannah would just pick up the phone and call the police ... *pick up the phone and dial 911, pick up the phone ....*

"*Gut himmel!*" Hannah stood in the doorway just behind the deacon. Her mouth was open and her eyes were wide.

Fantastic. That was just what they needed. Their last hope had stumbled in and was about to be captured too. They were all going to die—Emma, Kelly, Hannah, and David. There would be no one left to point the finger at the deacon.

"Everybody freeze!"

nineteen

Emma wilted with relief. A uniformed officer holding his gun at the ready stood to one side and slightly behind Hannah.

"Get down on the floor," a second officer ordered, "with your hands out in front of you."

David complied, and for a moment Emma thought Deacon Beachy might turn and run. But he lowered himself to his knees and lay down as instructed.

The first officer stepped aside as three others behind him filed into the room. He spoke into his two-way radio, then released Emma and Kelly from the belt that confined them.

Once they were free, rubbing their wrists where the thick leather had cut into their skin, Hannah launched herself at them, holding them both as close as she could as she rocked back and forth.

"I was so worried," she said, her voice muffled as her face was pressed into Emma's shoulder. "When I saw the deacon get out of the silver car, I was so scared." She released them to wipe tears from the corners of her eyes.

"How did the police get here?" Kelly asked.

Hannah held up Emma's cellphone, the one she had left in the console of the car after talking to Dottie Faye.

Emma sighed with relief. "I was worried that you wouldn't think to call."

"Or couldn't work the phone," Kelly added.

Hannah smiled. "I spent enough time with the *Englisch*

that I could figure it out. Though I think I might have erased half of your photographs." She bit her lip.

Emma shook her head. "You saved our lives."

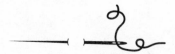

An hour and a half and three cups of bad coffee later, Emma, Kelly, and Hannah were finally allowed to leave the police station.

The deacon and David Wilson had been arrested for the murder of Alvin Lapp while the women gave their story of what happened.

"You'll inform the sheriff that the stable owner and the deacon have been arrested for killing Alvin?" Emma pressed.

The officer, a man who seemed too young to be carrying around a gun, nodded. He might be a little wet behind the ears, as Dottie Faye would say, but he exuded a confidence that put them all at ease.

Their statements taken, they were free to go.

The trio was taken back to the stables in another police car. Everyone was quiet as they turned into the parking lot. They thanked the officer and climbed into the Cadillac.

Emma laid her head against the headrest and closed her eyes. "What a day."

"You can say that again," Kelly murmured beside her.

"Why?" Hannah asked from the backseat.

"I suppose pressure can do that to a man." Emma sat up and reached for the keys.

In the rearview mirror, Emma could see Hannah shake her head. "Why would she say that again? One time is enough, *jah*?"

Emma and Kelly exchanged a look and burst out laughing. The stress of the day, of the week, had been overwhelming. It felt good to let it all out.

"I do not see what is so funny." Hannah crossed her arms.

"We'll explain on the way home." Emma smiled at her new friend and started the car.

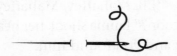

Everyone went to bed early that night. Between Dottie Faye's lingering headache and the excitement that Hannah, Emma, and Kelly had been through, extra rest was definitely in order. And much needed it seemed, for they barely made it downstairs the next morning in time to eat breakfast.

"Oh, Hannah." Sylvia rushed over as soon as she saw them. "I heard what happened yesterday. I am so sorry. Is there anything I can do?"

Hannah shook her head. "It is enough to know that I have been freed from suspicion."

Sylvia squeezed her hand. "You know where I am in case you need anything."

"*Jah*," Hannah said. "*Danki*."

They filled their plates and found a clean table just as the man with the cowboy hat finished his own meal.

"I was sure he was guilty." Dottie Faye shook her head.

The man turned and caught her staring at him.

Dottie Faye lowered her gaze, but it was too late. He was on his way over.

"Hey there, little lady," he said in a slow Texas drawl, tipping his hat to her. "I couldn't help but notice that … well, you seem to be watching me." He smiled, revealing twin dimples. He had to be in his late sixties, a perfect combination of urbane and rugged, like John Forsyth meets Sam Elliott. "Well, I'm headin' back to Texas today, but if you're ever in the area, you look me up, y'hear?" He handed her a business card. Then he flashed her a wink and sauntered out the door.

"Well, I'll be," Dottie Faye whispered, turning his card over in her hands. "'J.B. Mahaffey, Mahaffey Oil.'"

"He's an oil tycoon?" Emma shook her head. "One millionaire in the county and you found him."

Dottie Faye smiled. "It's a talent."

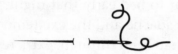

Without a new murder to solve and stalled in the quest to find out who killed Rose, the afternoon loomed ahead of them. They went back up to their suite. Emma got out the quilt blocks and spread them on the coffee table, allowing Hannah to look at them once again.

Hannah ran her fingers over the cloth, touching each block one by one.

Hannah stopped on her own block. "Troyer Amish aren't allowed to wear many bright colors. Some Amish put them in their quilts or plant red and yellow flowers out in front of their houses in order to add those colors to their lives."

"Is that why your block is so ... bright?"

Bright wasn't quite the word for the piece. *Neon, glaring*—adjectives like those were more accurate.

Hannah lightly fingered the stitches. "It's a buggy, you know."

Emma turned the piece toward her to get a better look at it.

"Here." Hannah traced the lines that made up a misshapen

square. "From the back. These are the wheels." She ran a finger down the vertical lines at each side of the square.

"I see it!" Kelly exclaimed.

Dottie Faye twisted her mouth this way and that, then finally gave up and sat back.

"It might have helped if you had put a caution triangle on the back," Emma suggested.

Hannah chuckled. "Rose said the same thing."

Hearing this, it was almost as if they had Rose there with them.

"I was in protest," Hannah explained. "I made my square to be the opposite of everything the Amish stood for. It is too bright, and the fabrics are ones that Amish would not be allowed to wear. Silk, velvet." She brushed her fingers across it again.

"If you didn't like what the Amish stood for, then why did you come back?" Dottie Faye asked.

Emma and Kelly both shot her a look.

"What?" Dottie Faye asked with a shrug.

"It is *allrecht*." Hannah pressed her hands into her lap as if she couldn't stand to touch the quilt any longer. "Do you know how hard it is to make it in the *Englisch* world?" She laughed. "Of course not."

"It's hard enough when you're English," Kelly said.

Hannah nodded. "I tried, but it seemed as if the longer I stayed, the more I did not fit in."

"Is that why your classmates said you were unhappy with Rose?" Emma asked.

"I was unhappy with everyone, but mostly with myself. I felt like a failure."

"And then you got a D in a Rose's class," Kelly added.

"Yes. Adding insult to pains. Is that what you say?"

"To injury," Dottie Faye corrected. "Insult to injury."

"*Jah*," Hannah said. "That." She pleated her fingers in the skirt of her drab dress. "I know it was immature, but it seemed as if Rose was proving to me that I didn't belong. But you know I didn't kill her. I could never."

"We know." Emma patted her on the knee. "Any of these names ring a bell?"

Hannah frowned.

"Bring to mind the person you saw Rose with the night before she fell?"

"Oh. *Nay*," she said. "I wish it did, though."

"Me too," Kelly murmured.

"Do you remember what he looked like?"

Hannah shrugged. "His hair wasn't blond, but it wasn't dark either. And he wasn't as big as Alvin." She closed her eyes as if trying to remember more.

"It's OK," Kelly said, gently touching her arm. "It was a long time ago."

Hannah opened her eyes with a sad smile. "I want so badly to remember. You have helped me so much. I want to give back to you."

Emma turned to Kelly. "We'll just have to pick a block and go on," she said. It was either that or give up. *That* wasn't something she could do.

"I know." Hannah clapped her hands together in glee.

"You know who Rose was with that night?" Excitement leapt inside Emma.

Hannah's expression fell. "I mean, I know what I can do for you to thank you for all that you have done for me."

Emma tried not to let her disappointment show. "Oh. And what is that?"

"I will cook for you tonight."

There went her waistline.

"The three of you can come to my home and stay the night," Hannah continued.

"Like an Amish sleepover?" Dottie Faye asked.

"*Jah*. I will cook for you. Afterward we can quilt and tell stories. You can see how we Amish live."

Dottie Faye looked around at their suite, then back to Hannah's expectant face.

Emma waited for her aunt to protest.

"Now that's what I was talking about." Dottie Faye rubbed her hands together. "The real Amish experience."

They packed up their bags that afternoon and said goodbye to the Yoder B&B. They thanked Casey for all her help, wished her well, and hugged her goodbye.

"I paid for her prom dress," Dottie Faye told Emma and Kelly as they left. "I have one more thing to do. You girls go ahead. I'll be right along."

When Dottie Faye took a little longer than Emma thought she would, she went back to check on her. Inside she found her aunt stuffing the collection box for little Joshua Beachy, the deacon's son. With his father certain to go to jail and most likely on to prison, the boy and his family were going to need all the extra money they could get.

"You're a real softie, you know that, Dottie Faye?"

"Like I told you before, a girl's gotta do what a girl's gotta do."

"I can't believe you really cook on that." Dottie Faye eyed the wood-burning stove dubiously.

"*Jah*," Hannah answered, her cheeks flushed pink with excitement and heat.

Hannah stirred a big pot of something that looked like soup, though she assured them it was chicken pot pie. Whatever it was, it smelled divine, and Emma couldn't wait to give it a try.

"It certainly smells good." Dottie Faye echoed Emma's thoughts.

Kelly nodded in agreement.

Hannah reached into the oven and pulled out a pan of sourdough dinner rolls. "This is my family recipe," she explained. "We have had this starter for five generations."

Dottie Faye good-naturedly elbowed Emma. "See? Traditions are cool."

Emma just smiled.

Hannah slipped her cherry pie into the warm oven. "Now that will cook while we eat. Are you *hungerich*?"

The trio nodded.

Hannah refused to let them do anything to help. Emma wondered if Hannah just wanted to give them special treatment or if she didn't like sharing her kitchen space with another set of hands.

They sat at the simple wooden table while she brought the food over to them along with a plethora of jars and a crock of thick cheese.

She sat down and smiled at her guests. It was the happiest Emma had seen her since they had met. "The Amish pray before and after every meal," Hannah explained.

"Do you want me to say grace?" Dottie Faye asked.

Hannah shook her head. "We pray silently, giving our individual thanks to God."

Everyone bowed their heads.

Emma said thanks for their safe trip to New York and

asked that God watch over them as they journeyed home the following day. With or without the name of the student Rose had been seen with, it was time for them to return to Mystic Harbor. She added her thanks for the food and that someone had looked out for them at the stables the day before. Then she asked the Lord to watch over Hannah. The poor woman had been through so much.

"*Aemen*," Hannah murmured. She looked up and once again smiled at her guests. "This is goat cheese," she said, handing the crock to Emma. "There are pickles, chow-chow, and relish on the table too. Oh, and applesauce if you are inclined. Everybody eat."

For a few minutes nothing could be heard but the clink of silverware against dishes. Then Dottie Faye broke the silence. "Hannah, this is delicious."

Emma and Kelly nodded their agreement. "So much better than the diner," Kelly said. Emma could only nod, her mouth too full to speak.

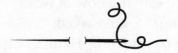

"That was wonderful," Emma said. They had eaten, prayed again, cleared the table, and washed the dishes.

Hannah didn't have indoor plumbing, so they had taken the dishes to the back porch and washed them in a sink with water heated in a wood-burning water heater. That wasn't so much of a chore, but Emma was not looking forward to using the outhouse. What an adventure this was turning out to be.

"My favorite was the goat cheese," Kelly said. "You could make a fortune on that. Don't you have a market where you could sell it?"

"I saw one at the edge of town," Dottie Faye said.

"That's right," Emma added. "We passed it on the way to meet the Mennonite driver."

Hannah nodded slowly. *"Jah.* I suppose."

"I'm telling you, you could make a killing off that cheese," Dottie Faye said.

Hannah's forehead buckled into a deep frown. "Why would I want to kill over cheese? That is terrible."

"That's not what it means," Emma said, quickly explaining the English meaning.

"Maybe even enough to earn a living," Dottie Faye added. "If you keep leasing your land and stuff."

Hannah's face brightened. "Maybe I could make pies again."

"You mean go up against Ben Lambright?" Emma asked.

Hannah nodded. "A little competition is a *gut* thing, *jah?*"

"I don't know, Hannah." Dottie Faye tapped her chin with one finger. "Ben the Baker's pies are pretty incredible."

"Wait till you taste mine." Hannah slapped a hand over her mouth as if to stay the flow of words.

"What's wrong?" Emma asked.

"It is a sin to be prideful," Hannah explained.

"Honey, it ain't pride if you can back it up." Dottie Faye looped one arm through Hannah's and led her back into the kitchen.

As predicted, when they were finished cleaning up, the pie was perfectly browned. Hannah took it from the oven and set it on the table to cool. "By the time we get the goats milked, the pie will be ready to eat. Then we can quilt until the sun goes down."

"Milk the goats?" Dottie Faye shot Hannah a horrified look. "I think I'll watch."

Emma, Kelly, and Hannah just laughed. That was just Dottie Faye, after all.

Hannah led them to the barn.

True to her words, Dottie Faye watched as Emma and Kelly tried their hand at milking the goats. In the end, Hannah did the milking, making short work of the three nannies she kept.

"I suppose if I want to make more cheese, I will need more goats," Hannah mused as she finished milking.

"Maybe you can use some of the money the deacon gave you," Kelly suggested.

Hannah got a thoughtful look and nodded.

"I don't know about you girls, but I gotta tinkle," Dottie Faye said.

Emma inwardly cringed. If her aunt didn't want to milk a goat, Emma was certain she wouldn't take the news of an outhouse well. Maybe they should have stayed in town.

But Hannah got a sparkle in her eyes and motioned for them to follow her. "Let me show you a secret." She led them through the stalls to what Emma would have called a tack room. It was filled with all sorts of tools and brushes, harnesses and other items needed for the care of farm animals.

"Through there." She pointed to a narrow door on the far wall of the room.

"There's a toilet in here," Dottie Faye announced. "And a sink with running water."

Hannah grinned. "But it is our secret, *jah*? The bishop would have a fit if he knew it was here."

Dottie Faye pretended to lock her mouth and throw away the key.

Hannah was lucky they were leaving tomorrow. Despite Dottie Faye's good intentions, Emma didn't think she could keep a secret more than two days.

"Come on," Hannah said after they had taken care of their business. "I'll show you how the Amish quilt."

twenty

"I thought we were going to eat pie," Dottie Faye grumbled as Hannah brought out a large quilting frame. They pushed the wooden bench that served as Hannah's couch to one side of the living room in order to take advantage of the natural light streaming in through the windows.

"If we want to quilt," Kelly said, "we have to do it before the sun sets."

"*Jah*," Hannah said. "The lanterns do not give enough light to do such things after dark."

"Lanterns?" Dottie Faye looked skeptical.

Emma hid her smile. This was the all-out Amish experience that Dottie Faye had talked about just days ago.

Hannah brought out a pristine white quilt backing. Emma and Kelly helped her stretch it across the wooden frame and clamp it into place.

"Now the blocks."

Exquisite wasn't quite the word for the stack of quilt blocks Hannah presented to them.

"This is called 'Sunshine and Shadow.'"

"We're familiar with the pattern," Emma said. "But your workmanship and the colors ...."

"They're gorgeous," Kelly added.

The quilt was composed of small squares of fabrics sewn together to create a fading fire of color on white. In the shape of a large diamond, the red, orange, yellow, and burgundy pieces all blended together to create a masterpiece.

"Wait a minute," Emma said, the recognition dawning. "Did you make the quilt in the window at Needles & Notions?"

Hannah flushed pink. "How did you know?"

"Something about the way you put the colors together. It's unique."

Hannah dropped her chin to her chest. "Is that *gut*?" she asked hesitantly.

"Good? It's fantastic. The most beautiful quilt I've ever seen."

Dottie Faye nodded in agreement. "No wonder you got your nose out of joint when Rose gave you a D."

Hannah frowned. "I do not understand what my nose has to do with it."

"She means that you were angry," Kelly explained with a smile.

"I was upset, but I learned a lot from Rose. I know what she was trying to do." She pointed to the far side of the quilt. "Now we each pick a side and start to work."

They gathered around the quilt and threaded their needles.

"What do you mean, you knew what Rose was trying to do?" Kelly asked as they stitched.

"She was a *gut* teacher, Rose. She knew I was struggling to survive in the English world. That D was her way of telling me to never stop trying harder. *Jah*, I might have been quilting longer than everybody in the class, but I should never stop trying to learn more."

"That's our Rose," Emma said with a smile.

"I just wish I was more help to you. You have done so much for me."

Emma did the best she could to hide her disappointment. She had hoped Hannah might remember who she had seen Rose with that night.

"What are you going to do now that you don't have a

new clue to chase down?" Dottie Faye asked.

Emma shrugged. "Go home and start again, I guess. There are four more blocks and names to research."

Hannah froze. "That is it!"

Kelly blinked in confusion. "What's it?"

Hannah jumped up, the quilt forgotten. "That is the name of the student Rose was with that night: Chase."

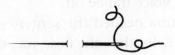

Emma unfolded the quilt blocks and laid them out across Hannah's dining table.

Hannah studied the blocks. "This one." She pointed to a square not quite perfectly sewn but composed of sophisticated colors and prints: a dark green plaid mixed with a midnight blue solid and a burgundy on burgundy floral. It was one of the nicest blocks on the piece, masculine and mature. Hannah turned over the square and pointed to the name on the back. "C. Meyer. That is why I did not remember it before. He signed it with his initial instead of his name."

Emma caught Kelly's gaze. It was disturbing enough to be told that their friend had been cozying up to a student in a pub, but to have that person's name was somewhat chilling. Could Chase Meyer be the murderer?

"It doesn't seem like Rose, does it?" Kelly asked.

Emma understood. Like her, Kelly had been hoping that Hannah was mistaken. "You're sure?" she asked.

"*Jah*, positive."

"But you didn't talk to them?"

Hannah shook her head. "They did not look like they wanted to be disturbed."

Emma's gaze met Kelly's again.

"They were not kissing," Hannah backpedaled. "But they were sitting really close. That I do remember."

Emma touched the square made by Chase Meyer one last time, then put away the blocks, placing them back into her bag for safekeeping.

"I remember because I did not think Rose was the type to ...." Hannah's voice trailed off.

Not that Emma needed the sentence to be complete. Neither she nor Kelly thought Rose was the sort of person who would date a student. Rose certainly never said anything to her or Kelly about it. They had grown up the best of friends. Was there something Rose had been trying to hide?

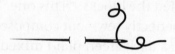

It was impossible to sit back down to calmly sew after Hannah's revelation. Instead, they left the quilt as it was and gathered around the table to eat pie.

The sun was setting, so Hannah lit the kerosene lamps. The flame threw a beautiful golden glow throughout the room.

"So this is your famous pie?" Dottie Faye asked.

Emma had vowed not to worry about calories on this trip, but old habits die hard. "Not such a big piece for me."

"Oh, eat up," Dottie Faye said. "You're looking a bit peaked."

Emma shook her head. "Peaked or not, I still have to fit in my clothes come tomorrow morning."

"I think you look just fine," Hannah said, but Emma noticed she cut her a smaller piece than everyone else.

"I never thought I would say this, but your pie is even better than Ben the Baker's," Dottie Faye said.

Even in the glowing light from the oil lamps, Emma caught Hannah's blush. "*Danki*, but I am not that *gut*."

Kelly shook her head. "I wouldn't be so sure about that."

"You know," Dottie Faye added, "you could sell these. Maybe the restaurant would buy from you. That'd sure help make ends meet."

"I have thought more about what I said about competition," Hannah said. "I do not think I could work against Ben Lambright. He has too many mouths to feed. His business is too important to his family."

"Then work for him," Kelly suggested.

"That's right." Emma snapped her fingers. "There was a 'Help Wanted' sign in the window last time we were there."

"Ben himself said he was shorthanded," Kelly said.

"I do not know," Hannah said. But Emma could tell the seed was planted. Working for Ben Lambright would help Hannah immensely. Their new friend was going to be just fine.

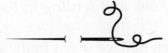

Hannah was up with the chickens and consequently, everyone else was too. After a big Amish breakfast—which completed their "total" Amish experience—Emma and Kelly packed the car.

"I do not know what I would have done without your help," Hannah said, giving each of them a hug. Her arms were stiff and her shoulders rigid, as if unaccustomed to the gesture. Still, she squeezed each of them tightly.

"I'm sure it would have worked out just fine, sugar." Dottie Faye patted her on the cheek.

"I want to show you my gratitude." Hannah motioned for them to follow her back into the house. Stacked on the table were three exquisite handmade quilts.

"These are for the three of you." She picked up the quilts one by one and handed them to Emma, Kelly, and Dottie Faye in turn.

"Oh, Hannah," Emma started. "This is too much."

But Hannah shook her head. "I have made many quilts in my lifetime, and I will make many more. I want you to take this to remember your time here in Fort Plain."

As if they could ever forget.

Kelly pulled two business cards from her pocket and handed them to Hannah. "One of these is our store in Mystic Harbor. The other belongs to a friend. If you ever want sell any of your quilts, she might be interested." She shrugged. "And if you just want to visit, now you know where we are."

"*Danki.*" Hannah walked them back outside.

Matthew Lapp pulled up in his buggy as they were putting the quilts in the back and settling in for the trip back to Massachusetts.

He waved, then hopped down from his seat to stand by Hannah as they backed out of the drive.

They waved in return.

Hannah smiled, and Emma couldn't help but notice they were leaving behind a much different Hannah than the one they'd first met. And as she would say, that was a *gut* thing.

twenty-one

"What do you think?" Emma shook out the Sunshine and Shadow quilt that Hannah had given her. She spread it over the racks so all the attending members of the Nimble Thimbles could admire it.

Everyone *oohed* and *aahed* over the cool purples and greens backed in the beige fabric the Amish call "paper bag."

"So this Amish girl wasn't the one?" Tokala asked, running her fingers across the perfect stitches.

"Nope." Dottie Faye shook her head. "But we know who might be."

Maeve Quigley frowned. The unspoken competition between Kelly's mother and Emma's aunt still burned strong. "Go ahead and tell them, Kelly."

They had taken a break from working on their individual projects to have some tea and cookies and share the story of their latest adventure. Emma knew Kelly's mom was a little put out that she had not been included in the trip, but Dottie Faye had proven to be an invaluable partner in crime fighting, and that was that. They hadn't left Maeve out intentionally.

"A man by the name of Chase Meyer," Kelly said.

Nods showed throughout the room, but Emma wasn't sure she wanted to divulge exactly *why* he was a suspect.

"It seems that he and Rose may have had a little something going on." Too late. Dottie Faye had already engaged her mouth before her brain.

"We don't know that, Dottie Faye," Emma admonished.

"We don't know if it isn't the truth either."

Emma couldn't argue with that, and yet ....

"So are you going to talk to this Chase Meyer person?" Marcia Goode asked from the doorway. Marcia owned Uncommon Threads, where the Nimble Thimbles met. She had obviously just popped in between customers and caught the end of what was going on.

"Of course," Dottie Faye said emphatically.

"We have to find him first," Emma said.

They had been home all of two days. Between getting the store settled, unpacking, and logging in everything they had learned from Hannah, Emma hadn't had time to do much else other than sleep.

"Marcia, we gave your card to Hannah Lapp," Kelly said. "I don't know if she'll call or not, but she makes fantastic quilts." Selling them this far from an Amish settlement would bring in a pretty penny.

"Is this one of hers?" Marcia stepped closer to the quilt, running her fingertips along the dusty diamond shapes. "Almost flawless." She touched the half-inch-long row of offset stitches toward the edge. "I heard that Amish women purposefully sew a mistake into their work so you know it's handmade. That's how perfect their stitches are."

But that would be prideful. Emma could almost hear Hannah say the words. "Actually, I asked Hannah about that. She said Amish women sew a delicately noticeable mistake into each quilt because nothing is perfect and everything is one of a kind."

She looked around the room at family and friends gathered around her. Each was one of a kind, special in his or her own way. Dottie Faye in her red leggings and navy blue and white sailor tunic in honor of Memorial Day; Maeve, ever polished and put together; Marcia, who, despite her best efforts, always seemed to have threads clinging to her; Tokala with her exotic looks; steady Walter; and dear Kelly.

All that was missing was Rose.

I'll find who killed you, my friend, Emma silently vowed. *No matter what it takes, I'll find him.*

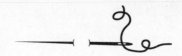

Mystery Sampler Quilt

Create your own mystery sampler quilt with blocks designed by
Emma and Kelly and inspired by each book in the series! You'll find
a Cotton & Grace block pattern in every Annie's Quilted Mysteries
book. At the end of the series, the last pattern will include finishing
instructions that will tell you how to stitch the unique blocks
together to create a beautiful, one-of-a-kind quilt.

Amish Star

Specifications
Finished Block Size: 12" x 12"
Skill Level: Confident Beginner

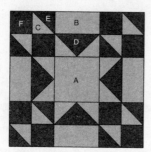

Amish Star
12" x 12" Finished Block

Cutting

From Light Fabric:
Cut 1 (4½") A square.
Cut 4 (2½" x 4½") B rectangles.
Cut 8 (2⅞") squares.
  Subcut each square on 1 diagonal to
  make 16 C triangles.

From Dark Fabric:
Cut 1 (5¼") square.
  Subcut on both diagonals to make 4 D
  triangles.
Cut 4 (2⅞") squares.
  Subcut each square on 1 diagonal to
  make 8 E triangles.
Cut 8 (2½") F squares.

Assembly

1. Stitch an E and C triangle together along long edge
(Figure 1); press seam toward E. Repeat to make eight
E-C units.

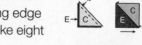

Figure 1

2. Stitch a C triangle to an angled side
of a D triangle (Figure 2); press seam
toward D.

Figure 2

3. Stitch a C triangle to opposite angled side of D to make a flying geese unit referring again to Figure 2. Repeat to make four units.

4. Stitch an F square to the C side of an E-C unit (Figure 3); press seam toward F. Repeat to make eight rows.

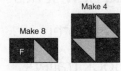

Make 8

Make 4

Figure 3

Make 4

B

Figure 4

5. Stitch two F-E-C rows together, referring again to Figure 3 for orientation, to make a corner unit; press seam to one side. Repeat to make four corner units.

6. Stitch a B rectangle to the D edge of a flying geese unit (Figure 4); press seam toward D. Repeat to make four B units.

7. Referring to Figure 5 to complete block, stitch corner blocks on opposite ends of a B unit to make a row; press seams toward B unit. Repeat to make a top and bottom block row. Stitch B units to opposite sides of A to make block center row; press seams toward A. Stitch rows together; press seams toward center row.

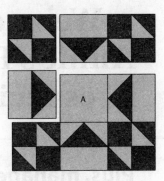

A

Figure 5

HELPFUL HINTS
• Choose light and dark fabrics for this block. Use scraps from other projects or purchase fat eighths (9" x 22") or fat quarters (18" x 22") to make one sample block.

• Cut individual pieces from scraps, or cut strips and then individual pieces from strips if using yardage or large pieces of fabric. For example, to cut several 2½" squares, cut a 2½"-wide strip the width of the fabric. Subcut the strip into 2½" squares.

• Use a ¼"-wide seam allowance for all seams and stitch right sides together.

Learn more about Annie's fiction books at

AnniesFiction.com

- Access your e-books
- Discover exciting new series
- Read sample chapters
- Watch video book trailers
- Share your feedback

We've designed the Annie's Fiction website especially for you!

Plus, manage your account online!

- Check your account status
- Make payments online
- Update your address

ANNIE'S ATTIC
MYSTERIES®

CREATIVE WOMAN
MYSTERIES®

Annie's
Quilted
Mysteries™

Annie's
Mysteries
Unraveled™

Visit us at AnniesFiction.com

COMING SOON!

SEAM OF THE CRIME

Emma and Dottie Faye team up with private investigator
Alex Manning as they head next to New York in
search of their next suspect, Chase Meyer.

Chase now works for Of Monsters & Men, an
animatronics firm that specializes in scary Halloween
props. But could a real monster be hiding there?

Don't miss the next book in this
exciting new series from
Annie's Quilted Mysteries!